KOSMIC KISS

KOSMIC
BOOK 2

ERIN KAY

COPYRIGHT

AN INTRO TO KOSMIC

KOSMIC (코스믹) is a 6-member male group under CKM Entertainment. The group consists of: Changmin, Byunho, Tai, Simon, Haru, Jaesung, and formerly Hajun (left the group due to a scandal in 2022). They debuted on June 11, 2019 with their song 'KOSMOS.'

KOSMIC Fandom Name: Infinity (plural: Infinities)

Changmin

Birth Name: Lee Changmin (이창민)
Position: Leader, songwriter/producer, rapper, vocalist
Birthday: June 13, 1997 (Zodiac: Gemini)
Height: 178 cm (5'10")
Blood type: AB
MBTI: ENTP

Byunho

Birth name: Seo Byunho (서 병호), also romanized Byungho
Position: Main rapper, lead dancer, songwriter/producer

Birthday: Oct 28, 1997 (Zodiac: Scorpio)
Height: 180 cm (5′11″)
Blood type: B
MBTI: ESTP / ISTP (he's gotten both results)

Tai

Birth Name: Sun Tai (孙泰)

Position: Main dancer, lead rapper, vocalist, songwriter/producer

Birthday: Jan 16, 1999 (Zodiac: Capricorn)

Height: 179 cm (5′10″)

Blood type: B

MBTI: INFJ

Hajun (Former Member)

Birth name: Yun Hajun (윤하준)

Position: Main dancer, main vocalist, center, songwriter/producer

Birthday: Aug 4, 1999 (Zodiac: Leo)

Height: 183 cm (6′0″)

Blood type: O

MBTI: ENFJ

Simon

Birth name: Jung Simon

Position: Main vocalist, visual, songwriter

Birthday: April 8, 2000 (Zodiac: Aries)

Height: 177 cm (5′10″)

Blood type: A

MBTI: INTP

Haru

Birth name: Yukimura Haru (雪村 晴)
  Position: Lead vocalist, main dancer
  Birthday: Oct 19, 2000 (Zodiac: Libra)
  Height: 175 cm (5'9")
  Blood type: A
  MBTI: INFP

Jaesung

Birth name: Park Jaesung (박 재성)
  Position: Vocalist, maknae, sub-rapper
  Birthday: Dec 17, 2001 (Zodiac: Sagittarius)
  Height: 172 cm (5'8")
  Blood type: O
  MBTI: ESFP

PROLOGUE

SKY

A year ago, I couldn't have predicted where I am now: sitting in a dressing room, preparing to greet one of the biggest K-Pop boy groups in the world—KOSMIC— as their new stylist.

The room is bright and filled with mirrors, racks and racks of designer clothes, and the smell of hairspray lingers in the air. I sit on one of a couple couches along the wall with the other stylists, the six of us (one lead stylist, three hair and makeup artists, and myself and the other assistant stylist) occupying ourselves with our phones or idle chatter while we wait. All of the preparation is done and our work doesn't start until the guys get here.

I was already a K-Pop fan when KOSMIC debuted, but they almost immediately became my favorite group. One random day in the library during my freshman year of college, I was procrastinating by watching YouTube and stumbled across their debut song "KOSMOS" in my recommendations. I clicked on it, and their music played in my headphones for the first time.

The music video introduced them as individual characters in a space-traveling future, with choreography interspersed throughout vibrant scenes of alien planets and space. The song itself was grungy and futuristic-sounding all at once. All of the members were gorgeous, but when Byunho came on the screen with his smoldering stare and sexy rapping voice, I couldn't resist doing a deep dive into the band, costing me some precious study time.

Because of a combination of coronavirus pandemic timing, school, and money, I never did get to see them in concert, but KOSMIC's songs filled my playlists and made the soundtrack to my life for the past several years.

It's a dream come true, sitting in a dressing room, waiting for my favorite band. Years of preparation have led to this moment. While doing fashion design school, I also took cosmetology classes, and after graduating, I did an internship in New York while waitressing on the side. For a while, I had no idea what I would do next.

But it turns out, my best friend from college was hiding a not-so-little secret from me.

When I was visiting Aera at her hotel in Manhattan a year ago, while she was there for a work trip, there happened to be someone else staying at her hotel: KOSMIC. That's how I found out that she's the daughter of their company's CEO. At the time, she was working as KOSMIC's assistant manager.

But Aera was also seeing one of KOSMIC's members, Hajun, and not long after their return to Korea, their relationship was revealed, causing a huge scandal which forced Hajun to leave the band. It's a long story, and not mine to tell.

Despite the conflict in her own life, Aera sent me the application for an assistant stylist position at CKM Entertainment and put in a good word for me. Most K-Pop stylists are older, married women and I'm neither of those things. I'm 24 years old and single. But Aera made the case that I should be on the company's style team because I would bring a "western perspective" to styling choices. Which was a smart way to sell me, because really, I don't have that much experience and my grasp of Korean isn't perfect.

After getting this job (thanks, best friend nepotism), I had a month of shadowing the other fashion and makeup stylists during another group's comeback– watching the choices and alterations that stylists made on the spot, every makeup and hair technique, and the process of preparing for a shoot or performance. I also continued the Korean language classes that I'd started in the U.S. during college, taking it more seriously now. I'm bilingual already because I grew up speaking English and Spanish, and have always been good with picking up languages, but that doesn't mean I'm able to learn anything instantly.

Not only has my first month and a half in Seoul been insanely busy, leaving little room to explore the country even though I would like to, but the culture shock has hit me harder than I expected. With my brown skin and curly black hair, I'm an obvious foreigner in a mostly homogenous country.

But now that I'm here living this incredible dream, the pressure is on me and the other stylists to prepare a stellar comeback look for the band. Although fashion is just one of the many facets that goes into a K-Pop comeback's success, this comeback is the first since Hajun's scandal and him leaving the band. I'm determined to do my part to make it successful.

A group of male voices floats down the hall leading into the dressing room. My stomach twists with nerves. And the six members of KOSMIC walk through the door.

PART 1

"'Cause in a sky, 'cause in a sky full of stars
    I think I see you"

— "Sky Full of Stars," Coldplay

ONE

 I'll melt your heart into two / I got that superstar glow"

— "Butter," BTS

SKY

THE HOTEL TOWERING above me shone in the afternoon sunlight, blindingly bright. The heat shimmered off the crowded Manhattan sidewalk. I followed my best friend Aera's petite figure into the lobby, taking a break from the outside heat to say goodbye to her within the air-conditioned indoors.

It was too bad that we didn't have time for anything more than a coffee date while she was back in the States. But I honestly didn't mind an excuse to come to NYC—I was a big city girl at heart. I wished that I'd been able to go to fashion school here, but it was too freaking expensive and I was paying for all of it by myself. Going to school in my home state of Massachusetts was the better option, at least until I could graduate and get an internship.

I pushed my black hexagon-framed sunglasses to the top of my head and let my eyes adjust to the indoor lighting, taking in shining marble floors and a sparkling crystal chandelier.

"Wow, your job really didn't skimp on your business trip. This hotel is really nice," I said, stalling by pretending to be interested in the lobby. I didn't know when I was going to be able to see Aera again. She worked in South Korea, where she was from. "Not that I'm surprised," I continued, trailing off—my eyes had snagged on a pair of handsome, well-dressed Asian men about thirty feet away, talking to the receptionist behind the desk.

Something about them was familiar enough to make my train of thought come to a stumbling halt.

One of them was taller than the other, with bright blue hair. The other had beachy, dyed brown hair. As I watched, the second one tapped the blue-haired one on the shoulder and gestured toward us, as if he'd noticed me staring. Then they were both looking in our direction.

An electric jolt went through me. I knew those faces. I'd seen them on my phone screen a thousand times. "Uh, Aera... Is that...Changmin and Hajun from the K-Pop group KOSMIC?" My voice turned high pitched at the end of the question, because they were still staring at us.

Aera spun around to see where I was looking, but I didn't get a response from her. The guys started striding in our direction.

Oh God. I wasn't that far from the exit. *Should I run away?* I thought.

They stopped a short distance from us and yep— those were definitely a couple of Korean pop stars. Each man was striking in his own way. Changmin, the brown-haired one, was like a prince, elegantly beautiful. Hajun, the one with blue hair, was simply magnetizing. I couldn't stop staring.

But what was weirder than seeing them in person was when Changmin said something (in Korean) to Aera. And she responded quickly and easily—like she talked to celebrities every day.

I glanced between them, clueless.

"Nice to meet you," Hajun said in slightly accented English. Was he talking to me? He was looking at me. "I'm Yun Hajun."

Like I didn't know who *Yun Hajun from KOSMIC* is.

He held his hand out to me to shake.

Was I hallucinating?

Head spinning, I prayed my hand wasn't sweaty and placed my palm in his. His hand was warm and smooth. We shook, making eye contact. Eye contact! With *the* Yun Hajun!

He was, without a doubt, the most perfect human being I'd ever laid eyes on in person—strong jaw, full lips, flawless skin, taller than me by a good several inches even in heels. And he was just one of the seven of them.

"I'm... um..." What was my name again? Hajun's mouth twitched as if he was trying not to laugh at my reaction to meeting him. "Sky."

I shook myself out of my trance and turned to Aera. This girl had some explaining to do. "What. Is. Happening," I whispered, probably too loudly. "Am I dreaming? How the hell do you know K-Pop idols? Did I just shake Yun Hajun's hand?" I cut myself off before I could continue my stream of questions.

"It's complicated," Aera said.

Seriously? My friend had always been secretive about her life, but this was too much to brush off. I resisted the urge to grab her shoulders and shake the answers out of her.

But as they exchanged a few more words in Korean, it all clicked into place. Aera was here on a business trip. KOSMIC, I knew, were here in the U.S. promoting their new album.

"Oh my god!" I blurted. "Your job. You work for them.

You're here because of them." I waved a hand at the two idols in front of us.

"We work for her," Hajun corrected. I didn't miss the familiar irritated look Aera gave him, but my mind was still processing what he said.

Worked *for* her.

It'd been obvious to me since we were roommates at Harvard that Aera's family had money, her designer clothes being the most obvious giveaway. My family wasn't poor, but we were still middle class. I always sort of figured, there must be some other reason she didn't tell me much about her past. "Businessman" was always as specific as she would get about her dad, and I never pushed, because I knew she had a complicated relationship with him. She never went back home during school breaks, so instead of spending the holidays alone, I would bring her home to spend them with my family.

Now it all made sense. If her family's business was in the K-Pop entertainment industry, she wouldn't tell people because her life existed in such close proximity to K-Pop idols. And there were some creepy K-Pop stans out there.

"This is insane. That's why you could never tell me what your family does," I said, realizing after a second that I spoke my thoughts out loud.

Changmin and Hajun glanced at each other and in some unspoken agreement, retreated to several paces away, giving us some space. Aera's shoulders were tense and her expression guarded, like she expected me to be upset with her for keeping this secret.

I rushed to reassure her. "I don't blame you. How would you know who's a real friend and who just wants to get close because of who you know? But this is really cool. I can't believe you know KOSMIC. Your family really owns CKM Entertainment. That's unbelievable." My thoughts kept spilling out of my mouth in a combination of shock and excitement.

She nodded, confirming my wild guess, looking relieved but still wary. "Yeah." I sensed her putting up a wall, and the last thing I wanted to do was leave, but she obviously had some work to do and hadn't meant for me to find out about her connection to KOSMIC. Probably because everyone reacted the way I did, I realized. Oh god, was *I* being a creepy fan?

I definitely didn't want to be like that. "Okay, I'll go. Um. This is just a lot." I snuck another glance at Hajun and Changmin, who were the living definition of *a lot*. Standing there talking casually with each other, they still managed to look effortlessly attractive.

To my surprise, Aera sighed and said, "Come with me. You can meet the rest of the members."

How could I say no to that?

* * *

THE ELEVATOR RIDE UP to where the KOSMIC members were staying was... awkward. There was some strange tension hanging in the air, and Aera, who had seemed distracted since the moment she showed up for coffee, seemed even more distracted than before. She and Hajun kept sneaking glances at each other—which was interesting.

But I didn't have the mental space to contemplate it right now, because I was too busy panicking about the fact that I was about to meet other members of my favorite K-Pop band.

Thank goodness I had a cute outfit today—that always helped to boost my self-confidence. I was wearing a short-sleeved, tangerine orange frilled top that I'd made with a mid-thigh-length black faux leather skirt and some black open-toe, chunky-heeled ankle boots. My toes were painted a matching

5

sunset orange, and my hair was slicked back into a ponytail with a few loose curls framing my face. I stood up a bit straighter.

Despite the awkwardness saturating the air in the elevator, I spoke up. "I love the new album," I told Changmin. Famous superstars liked to talk about their music, right? Seemed like a safe bet.

KOSMIC's leader flashed me a dazzling smile, showing the dimple in his cheek. "Thank you," he said, and his whole response seemed so genuinely pleased that my face flushed.

"I was at the filming for their new music video ADRIFT on my first day," Aera told me casually.

My jaw dropped. "That's so cool." I had watched the premier of that music video, which had such amazing CGI it could have been from a science fiction film. I remembered drooling over some of the members' dystopian-looking outfits. And how good Byunho had looked in that video.

My bias, who I might be just about to meet.

The elevator dinged, announcing our arrival at the floor where KOSMIC was staying. My heart began thumping against my ribs so hard I thought I might be having a heart attack.

"Let's see who's awake for you to meet," Aera said, but at that very moment, there was a sudden commotion as the two youngest members of KOSMIC raced around the corner of the hallway toward us, followed by—

Seo Byungho.

He was yelling something and looked extremely annoyed. I gawked at him, wondering how it was possible for a person to get more attractive when angry.

Changmin intervened and stopped Jaesung by stepping in front of him. He snatched a blue elephant plushie out of his hands and passed it to Byunho.

I realized that the two maknaes must have stolen Byunho's elephant plushie.

My favorite K-Pop rapper has a blue elephant plushie. Did he cuddle with it at night? Aww. That would be way too cute.

Seeing his audience, Byunho scowled and moved the plushie behind his back, hiding it from view. Then he addressed Aera in Korean. She responded before adding in English, "Byunho, this is my friend Sky."

My bones turned to Jell-O as my bias turned his attention to me. He was famous for that smoldering look, with those dark, heavy eyebrows and intense gaze—but I wasn't prepared for the full force of feeling it not just through a screen, but in person.

His gaze flickered over me, stealing my breath away and setting all of my nerve endings tingling like I'd stuck my finger into an electrical outlet.

"H-hello," I managed to stutter before the silence got too long and weird. My palms were sweating. *Say something else, Sky!* "You're my favorite rapper," I blurted.

Oh, I could die from embarrassment.

"Hello. Thanks for your support of our music," Byunho said, his accent making his English thicker, but still clearly understandable. His voice was so deep in person that I got that full body, shivering sensation again.

There was something so unreal about standing in front of him. My adoration of him was so powerful, that being perceived by him made me feel as if I were meeting a god. I couldn't breathe.

Then he wasn't looking at me anymore, and I could sort of breathe again. He said something in Korean to Changmin before striding off in the direction he came, carrying his blue elephant with one hand by his side.

Next I was introduced to the youngest members, called maknaes in Korean. Haru and Jaesung were even more charming in person despite the fact that we couldn't understand each other well—they asked me about my favorite foods ("I don't eat meat," to which they responded with shock) and expressed to me their undying love of New York City pizza. The interaction was so enjoyable that I didn't notice the band's manager showing up and telling Aera that I couldn't be here, until she took my hand and muttered an apology in my ear before leading me away.

As we took the elevator back downstairs, I was grinning like an idiot. Meanwhile, Aera frowned at the elevator door as if it had insulted her.

"That's the stupid manager who made me late for our lunch date even though I asked for the time off."

"How dare he," I agreed, as the elevator dinged for the lobby. She grabbed my hand and pulled me toward the nearby stairwell.

She was taking me back upstairs, even though that was clearly against the rules.

This side of Aera was kind of scary, honestly, since she was normally the opposite of hotheaded. "Are you sure this is okay?"

"What's he going to do, fire me?" She laughed. It was kind of evil sounding, but I had a sense of self-preservation, so I didn't point that out. "Like he said, I'm the chairman's daughter."

We took the stairs until we reached the third level, which was reserved entirely for KOSMIC and their crew. After some peeking around corners and sneaking past guards (pretty challenging in heels), we made it to her room.

Aera let out a long sigh after shutting the door behind us.

I sat down on the edge of her hotel bed, which looked like it'd been freshly made by room service. Then, my thoughts started spilling out of me. "I can't believe any of this. I've been a fan for years but I never thought anything like this could happen."

Meeting KOSMIC. Meeting Byunho. My heart swelled with happiness. This was a memory I would treasure forever.

Aera shocked me out of my reverie by wrapping her arms around my shoulders in a tight hug. She'd never been the most touchy-feely person. "I missed you so much," she said.

I squeezed her back and then pulled away, smiling at her. "I missed you, too." We met our first year at Harvard, when we were paired up as roommates. Right away, I could tell she was lonely and that she always held herself at a distance from others, but circumstances and the horrors of freshman year brought us together. Even when I dropped out of business school to go to fashion school—the toughest time of my life because my family was completely against it—we stayed friends through it all.

"I tried to hide this, my life and my connections, for so long," she said, looking down at her hands clenched in her lap. "That's why I had no Korean friends at school." It was true, I never even heard Aera speak Korean when we were at uni together, let alone see her interact with other Korean international students. She must have been worried about getting attention because of who she was. "Now that you know, I don't know whether to feel relieved, or angry that the one safe part of my life is being affected by it."

I studied my friend's face, trying to put myself in her shoes, to understand what her life must be like. It was strange, that we were friends for four years and still, I didn't know her secret life. "I don't know what that's like. I can only imagine. But I promise that nothing between us is going to change. It's cool to meet celebrities, but I've always thought you were the coolest person in my life. My best friend." I meant it.

Aera pulled me into another hug. We stayed like that for a moment, as my mind drifted to something that had been nagging at my curiosity ever since she mentioned it. Since all the secrets were coming out now, this was my chance to ask.

"I am curious about one thing though," I said. "And maybe this is stupid of me to ask... You told me you made out with one of your coworkers before... you couldn't mean..." I widened my eyes meaningfully. She had hinted at something happening with someone she worked with, which could mean...

"Yun Hajun," she said.

I jumped up in shock, a loud squeak of excitement slipping out of me. Aera shushed me, and I smothered my grin with my hand. "Are you fucking serious? Holy shit, girl. That man is..."

Aera blushed. Actually *blushed*. I don't think I'd ever seen her react to a man with any expression other than disgust or indifference. And then, she admitted, "I slept with him last night."

This was too much. "YOU DID NOT." I had to pace across the room to collect myself. I looked back at my blushing friend with disbelief. Other incoherent noises came out of my mouth, but I managed to repeat several more times, "You did not!" I took a deep breath, trying to stop losing my shit. "You have to tell me what happened from the beginning."

With an equally deep breath, Aera began the story of meeting Hajun just after her high school graduation, in the practice rooms at CKM Entertainment. How she had misled him to think she was a trainee there, like him, so that they could continue meeting in secret. And when they were discovered by several other trainees, Aera was sent away to the U.S. for college and not allowed to return home.

"That's messed up," I said. "No wonder you were so emo freshman year."

She rolled her eyes. "Anyway, KOSMIC debuted not long after I left."

Come to think of it, whenever they had come up in conversation or a song of theirs played, I thought Aera disliked

KOSMIC because she would change the subject or make an excuse to skip the song. It all made so much sense now.

And when Aera went back to South Korea, her father wanted her to get some experience with artist management, forcing her to be in close proximity with Hajun. And Hajun, simply put, wouldn't let her forget what happened between them. From what Aera said, it sounded like he could be very persuasive.

"You lucky bitch," I said affectionately, when she was finished describing the series of events that had led her and Hajun to the sort of situationship they were in right now.

Aera, cheeks still pink, checked her gleaming silver watch. "We have to get to the airport now. More promotions in Los Angeles." She sighed.

"I'll see you off downstairs," I promised.

* * *

AS WE WERE HUGGING goodbye in the lobby, I gave Aera some discreet encouragement. "Get it, girl," I whispered in her ear. She giggled and blushed.

Byunho walked past us with his suitcase, his dark eyes snagging on mine for a second. I looked down quickly.

I waved goodbye to my best friend and my favorite band, not knowing that in just a year, I would be seeing them all again.

TWO

NOW

 Starlight, starlight / With you shining in my mind"

— "Star," LOONA

BYUNHO

FOLLOWING our recording session we only have enough time to eat some dietician-approved protein bars on our way to the fitting session for this comeback. After almost a year of hiatus to work on personal projects, it's jarring to be back to our old routine, especially because it's the first time we're doing it all without Hajun.

Before long, I'll be on stage again. Most of our activities during our hiatus weren't music-related—we took more intensive English lessons and did individual activities, but the only real group project was a science fiction movie we filmed. It's a sequel to one we released just after our debut and is set to be in theaters at the end of the year. I released a mixtape six months into hiatus but didn't get the chance to promote it. I'm itching to perform again.

So while being forced to try on clothes I would never choose to wear, being poked and prodded and painted with makeup is my least favorite part of being an idol, I can deal with it as a minor inconvenience. I'm determined to put up with it.

But then, as I enter the dressing room, I see *her*. My steps halt, and Jaesung stumbles into my back.

"Sorry, hyung!" he yelps, darting out of reach—but my attention is on the woman whose brown eyes are now on mine. A jolt of familiarity goes through me. I break eye contact.

I remember her, from that day in the hotel in New York. The fan who is a friend of Kim Aera's.

What is *she* doing here?

SKY

Byunho is the first one to notice me. It's like my eyeballs are magnets for his tall, lean frame, and he immediately catches me staring. Almost as quickly as our eyes meet, he looks away from me.

Ms. Goh, the lead stylist, starts giving rapid-fire instructions to the staff members that I partly miss because I'm distracted by Byunho. I scramble to catch up.

I follow the other stylists' lead and hurry to the nearest clothing rack. I select Changmin's first music video outfit in a clothing bag, labeled with his name (thankfully, learning to read Hangul was the easy part of learning Korean), and approach him with it slung over my arm.

The leader of KOSMIC does a double take, then gives me a dazzling smile of recognition that warms my skin like sunshine. "You're Kim Aera's friend, Sky, right?" Changmin asks in English. "I knew we were getting a new stylist, but I didn't know it was you. Welcome to the team."

"Kamsahamnida," I murmur, giving a shy bow.

"Hey, guys! It's Aera's friend from New York!" Changmin says loudly in Korean to the other guys. "Come say hello."

Suddenly, the group of guys is crowded around me. Haru and Jaesung clearly remember me, Jaesung grinning ear to ear and Haru smiling shyly. Changmin explains to them that I'm the new stylist and introduces me to Tai and Simon.

Tai gives me a polite smile that doesn't quite reach his eyes. Maybe Aera is still a sore spot for the members, since the scandal with her is what caused Hajun to leave the band. I didn't think of this before, but it's possible my association with her will make things awkward.

"Pleasure to meet you," Simon says, his British accent as posh and charming as the slight smile he gives me.

Byunho's eyes catch mine, and my heart leaps into my throat.

"This isn't social hour. Time to work," Stylist Goh reminds all of us, giving me a pointed look as she gives Tai the first outfit he must try on.

I hold the clothing bag out to Changmin. "Your first fit. Please try it on and we'll see how it looks."

Changmin flashes his dimple in an answering smile and takes the bag, before heading to one of the changing stalls.

I go back to the rack and check the labels, finding the outfit that each member needs to try on first. I grab Byunho's, determined not to be nervous about talking to him.

Byunho is leaning against the wall, looking at his phone.

"Hi. We, um, met before."

The rapper looks at me. "I remember you."

Okay, then.

He gestures to the garment bag in my arms. "That's for me?"

"Yes! I made it. Well, I made alterations to the original item. I've been assigned to style you for this comeback." Actually, I asked to put together his look book. Since Stylist Goh had to let me do something, I got the assignment. But now that I'm facing my subject, I feel frazzled and intimidated. I smile awkwardly as the silence stretches for a beat too long.

"Can I try it on?" Byunho asks, raising a brow at the fact that I am still possessively cradling the outfit he's supposed to wear to my chest.

"Oh! Yeah, here you go." I hold out the bag, and he takes it from me, brushing my upper arm with his hand in the process. My skin prickles.

"Thanks." Byunho heads toward the changing area.

I release a long breath and wipe my sweaty palms on my jeans.

BYUNHO

The first outfit that Sky designed are black, baggy coveralls with red accent stitching on the pockets and seams, and a plain black belt cinching the waist. I don't hate it.

The next two hours are a blur of changing clothes every ten minutes and my new stylist humming under her breath as she records notes on her phone and makes small adjustments to the outfits with pins. She avoids looking at my face and the few times she does, she drops her phone, pokes herself with a pin, and gets snapped at by Stylist Goh for moving too slowly.

By the end of it, I'm tired, hungry to the point of lightheadedness, and annoyed. How can I work with a stylist who's too timid to look at me?

As the session wraps up and it's time for us to go to the studio for some final touches on the album, I approach Stylist Goh. "If it's possible, I'd like to work with Eunjung-sshi again. I don't think the new stylist is working well with me."

If she's too nervous around me, I'll do us both a favor and

work with the assistant stylist who styled me for our last comeback.

Stylist Goh clicks her tongue. "Right now, I don't think it's possible. Eunjung has too much to do with other members."

I nod, accepting it with an inward wince. I'll just ignore the awkwardness, then, and hopefully Sky will get used to being around me.

Simon calls me from the door. "Hyung!"

SKY

Inside the changing stall, collecting outfits from the fitting and putting them back on hangers and in garment bags, I overhear Byunho's voice.

I listen in frozen silence as Byunho asks Ms. Goh not to work with me anymore. My Korean still isn't the best, but I understand it well enough that there's no mistake what he's asking.

It's been only a few hours and he already doesn't want to work with me.

For the first time, it occurs to me that my bias might actually be kind of a jerk in real life.

* * *

LATER THAT NIGHT, I'm sitting on the beanbag in my tiny studio apartment in Itaewon, eating takeout and watching Netflix on my laptop with a fan pointed at me to combat the humid heat of summer. The air is as thick and heavy as the thoughts within my head, mainly centering around my K-Pop bias and my job, and I barely have an appetite for the Indian food I ordered.

Maybe it's not fair to expect my ultimate bias to like me just because I like him. I mean, it's not like I actually *know* him. I just thought I did, in that highly delusional parasocial relationship way.

I think back to the first time I met him. The blue elephant plushie in his hand. Heartless jerks don't own cute stuffed animals, right? And the deeply introspective lyrics he often writes don't seem to fit with the idea that he's nothing but an arrogant celebrity.

Why would he ask Ms. Goh not to work with me? Is there just something about me that he can't stand? Honestly, I was a mess today, so I get it. But still. It's not like I'm a crazy fan. I was professional. His reaction feels way too harsh.

My phone rings, startling me out of my thoughts, "Mom" flashing on the screen. I pause the show and swipe to answer the FaceTime call.

Mom's face appears on the screen, her wide smile loosening some, but not all, of the knots in my stomach. "How are you, baby girl?" She still calls me that even though I'm 24. "How's the other side of the world?"

I rub my eyes, hoping they're not teary and that I don't look too pathetic in general. "I was just watching a show and eating dinner. Isn't it really early for you?"

"I just woke up, but I wanted to see your face before you go to bed."

I bring the phone right in front of my face. "There you go. How's that?"

She giggles. "I can see up your nose. Is that a hair?"

"Don't joke about that!" I squeak, but then I'm giggling too. "How are you and papa? And Tony?" Tony is my little brother, who's a junior in high school and wants to be a veterinarian.

"Working a lot, but good." My parents own a small law practice in a town north of Boston. "Your papa's knees are bothering him again, but he's starting physical therapy soon.

Tony won a science prize at school. But I called to hear about you! How is your job?"

I sigh. "It was my first day working with the members of KOSMIC today, and... I guess they aren't like I thought they would be in real life."

"What do you mean?"

"Like, I had this idealized version of them in my head. Even when I met them before, I still had this idea they were perfect angels because I was so starstruck by them. But I guess I'm really realizing that they're..." I trail off. They're people who know I exist and therefore have the opportunity to dislike me—though I'm not going to tell her about that.

Mom makes a noise of sympathy. "I think that's normal. Celebrities are probably not how they appear on camera."

I don't think she totally gets it, because she doesn't realize the emotional attachment that I have to KOSMIC.

"Oh! Your papa is up." She turns the screen to show my papa wrapped up in his bathrobe, yawning with a coffee mug in hand. He brightens when he sees me.

"Buenos días, international fashion star!"

"It's night time." I laugh at his enthusiasm.

He smacks his forehead. "Ah! Right. I forgot."

Mom points the phone back at herself. "We need to get ready for work, so I have to go, baby girl. Sleep well."

"Have a good day." I wave.

"We love you!" Papa chimes in from the background.

"Love you too."

A wave of homesickness crashes over me as I end the call, making my throat tight.

I'd been lucky to have a good childhood, with parents who loved me and each other. My father is Hispanic and my mother is Black. They'd met during law school in Louisiana. After law school they got married and moved to Massachusetts, where they bought a house with brick walls covered in ivy and a small garden in the backyard, and that's where I grew up. After getting accepted to Harvard, I was expected to follow in my parents footsteps, go to law school, and inherit their law firm. My future seemed more like a destiny. Maybe I can relate to Aera more than she realizes.

But at the beginning of my sophomore year, I realized that's not what I wanted to do. Since playing dress up as a child and learning to make my own clothes as a hobby all throughout middle and high school, I dreamed of designing beautiful clothing.

My parents were shocked when I told them I wanted to drop out of college and pursue that instead. They resisted. To make sure I was really committed to fashion design, they told me I'd have to pay for it on my own. They were only worried my dream wouldn't work out and that I was foolishly throwing away the education that I'd worked so hard for. Maybe fashion was just a childish hobby that I was never able to let go of.

If I'm being honest with myself, I worry about that too. And now that I am all the way across the world, heart heavy with homesickness, I try not to wonder if they were right.

THREE

> " I'm a bit of a bad boy, having bad habits / I'm a black hole"
>
> — "Black Hole," P1Harmony

SKY

I MEET Aera for breakfast before work the next morning at a cafe. She buys our drinks and an array of sweet pastries and we nestle into a cozy corner, surrounded by potted plants and the aroma of coffee beans. Due to our busy schedules, we haven't seen each other for almost a week.

"How did meeting the group yesterday go?" she asks me, pulling down her face mask to sip at her iced coffee.

"Good!" I lie cheerfully, taking a long slurp of my own iced peppermint latte. As much as I would like to tell her about Ms. Goh and Byunho, she's also the one who got me the job, and I don't want to complain. Especially not when she's dealing with so much on her own. "How about you?"

"There are so many things that need to change about the

way our company operates. I'm getting pushback, which makes everything more difficult. But progress is happening, albeit slowly." Aera sighs.

"What's going on with... you know." I glance around at the other customers.

The only one paying attention to us is Aera's bodyguard, a huge man sitting a couple tables away, that her father hired to follow her around everywhere ever since she started receiving death threats. But Gwan Jung doesn't speak English, and he's sworn to protect Aera's privacy.

When a photo of Aera and Hajun together got leaked to the press, the company had to terminate Hajun's contract with KOSMIC to "protect their public image." Hajun gets to stay with the company as a soloist, but that's little consolation. KOSMIC has barely been active as a group since then, only now coming back with their first group album since the scandal.

The members all had their own solo activities during that time. Changmin and Byunho released mixtapes, while Simon released a solo mini-album, Jaesung MCed at a music show, and Haru did some voice acting for a popular Japanese anime show. There are also rumors that they filmed a sequel to their first science fiction movie. I remember watching that movie over and over again when it came out, amazed by the special effects and their acting abilities... especially Byunho, playing a morally gray character with a cybernetic eye and arm.

I wince and push the thought of him from my mind.

A couple months ago, right after I got to Korea, Hajun released his first solo album. He and Aera spoke to each other for the first time since the scandal and have started dating again.

A smile curves Aera's mouth at the mention of Hajun, and her eyes soften. "It's good. We went for a drive outside the city this past weekend and had a picnic on top of a mountain. He's still busy promoting his album, and he's already working on the next one. But we try to see each other often."

"That's great. I'm happy for you." I reach across the table and squeeze her hand. There's something so heart-warming about the idea that my best friend might get the happily ever after she deserves after everything she's been through. It's hard not to feel a little envious, but I'm not stupid enough to let my own self-pity, that I don't have what she has, hurt our friendship.

BYUNHO

It's day one of our music video shoot for our new single, "ASTEROID." I'm reminded of another day, over a year ago, the day that Kim Aera showed up on the set of our last music video shoot.

Even though Hajun and I didn't get along a lot of the time, I can't ignore the expectation that when I turn my head, he'll be there flashing his irritating smirk. Nor can I ignore the nagging sensation of wrongness when he's not.

We're filming at an elaborately constructed set built within a giant warehouse. The set is meant to resemble a meteor crater, which involves a ton of gravel and larger rocks. Dry ice machines create smoke that drifts around the edges of the crater. An artificial alien jungle with electrically-powered neon plants surrounds the crash site. A green screen will create the backdrop behind the rest of the set.

"Whoa, daebak," Jaesung says, awed by the sight. But something about the concept bothers me.

"This is grim, isn't it?" Tai asks, apparently seeing what I do: the irony of this depiction in our first comeback since Hajun's scandal.

"I feel like we're looking at our career," I remark dryly.

Changmin cuts me a look. I chuckle silently but take the point to keep my unhelpful snark in check.

To be honest, our career has been the opposite of smooth. At first, our debut date kept getting pushed back, and then, when we finally debuted, the pandemic hit. We only had a couple good years of activity before Hajun's scandal with Aera broke, and then we were on hiatus from releasing music for almost a year. Now, we have only a short window of time before Changmin and I have to go to the military. So we have to make this comeback work.

Our new manager, Sangjin, directs us toward the large tent that's been set up for the stylists. I take a deep breath, preparing myself to deal with the nervous new stylist again, before I duck inside.

SKY

I move the handheld clothing steamer across some clothes hanging from the clothing rack, steaming out the wrinkles on them—these are the second outfits for the shoot, but Ms. Goh asked me to start getting them ready. I'm so lost in my task that I don't notice the man beside me until he clears his throat.

"Hello," Byunho says. I glance up and nearly drop the steamer on my foot.

Since I last saw him, he's had his hair styled for this comeback. His long, almost shoulder-length hair has been dyed a vibrant scarlet red and cut shorter in the front, longer in the back. Because I'm only an assistant fashion stylist, I don't have any say in what the hair stylists do—Ms. Goh is the mastermind behind coordinating all of that. And she's damn good at her job.

Byunho is so drop-dead gorgeous that I fully forget how to speak for a moment.

A frown crosses his face, snapping me out of my trance.

"Could you help zip this?" he asks, gesturing to his futuristic-looking metallic gray tunic, which has a high, stiff collar and zips in the back. From the scowl on his face, it's as if he resents asking me for help.

I bristle on the inside. "Of course," I say with a forced smile, turning off the steamer and setting it down on the nearby table. The other stylists and makeup artists are busy getting the other members of KOSMIC ready and starting on makeup.

I move behind Byunho and zip the tunic closed, my fingers accidentally brushing against the dip of his lower back. I quickly jerk my hand back and step away to survey the fit.

He looks like the hot villain from a Star Wars film—which is to say, he looks fantastic. I gesture toward the table and chair with the makeup setup. "Let's get your accessories and makeup done."

I'm not hired as a makeup artist—we have three employees on our team specifically assigned to hair and makeup—but I am expected to help out, since there are six members and the faster we get them all ready, the better. I would be excited to do makeup for an official shoot if I weren't so nervous around this guy.

As he sits down, I go to the accessory organizer hanging on the rack nearby and pick out several chunky steel rings and a black, star-shaped stud for his ear—nothing colorful, since this fit is monochromatic. I pass him the rings and watch as he slides them onto his long fingers one by one. My stomach does a strange little flip.

I need to put the stud in his ear.

My skin prickles with heat as I tentatively brush his hair out of the way. How is it possible for a man to have such nice skin? I gently grasp his earlobe, sliding the stud into his piercing and then screwing the back on, holding my breath the entire time.

"Do I make you nervous?" Byumho asks in a low voice, looking at me out of the corner of his eye.

I freeze at the question, considering several responses but settling on none. After what he said about not wanting to work with me, I don't know what to think about Seo Byunho. There's something gut-wrenching about realizing someone you idolized for years may not like you after meeting each other in real life.

The silence vibrates between us.

A muscle jumps in his jaw and he turns his head to face me. "If we're going to work together, you need to speak to me."

My stomach twists, and the words fall out of my mouth. "I heard you talking with Ms. Goh."

Byunho looks caught off guard for the first time since I've met him, his dark brows coming together. "You heard that?"

BYUNHO

Sky nods. It's as if speaking to her directly has finally broken the spell of her quiet restlessness, her flitting gaze and hesitant touches. She's looking me in the eye for the first time today, chin tipped up in slight defiance. "Yeah. I did." Frowning, she puts her hands on her hips, the motion drawing my attention to the way her jeans hug her curves. I snap my attention back to her face.

"I didn't mean it that way." I had no idea her Korean was good enough to understand, nor that she was nearby when I said it.

"What way?" Sky's voice is subdued, calm, but her brown eyes flash with a hurt that is then quickly concealed, like a door slammed shut in my face.

She calls to a makeup artist passing by. "He needs his makeup done."

Sky walks away before I can say another word to her.

Since I've met Sky, all I've done is embarrass myself and offend her. Fuck. I'm a total asshole.

* * *

"WHAT'S ON YOUR MIND, HYUNG?" Haru asks me one evening a couple days later as we make dinner for the other members together. Haru is as in his element in the kitchen as he is when he's dancing and singing.

Usually, it's him, Tai, and myself who do the cooking. Jaesung only knows how to make ramyun, and Simon only makes bland western food when asked to make anything–so we never ask, which I think is his intention. And Changmin's dishes have a tendency to be inedible no matter how hard he tries. We all can afford to order food from a restaurant every night, but we try to cook for ourselves at least one night a week when we're not on tour.

I'm frying the pork while Haru prepares the banchan—side dishes. I have my long hair tied in a ponytail back from my sweaty face, the heat in the kitchen almost intolerable after an eight-hour-long, already hot day shooting–and that's a relatively short day for us. At Haru's question, I glance over at him and raise a brow.

"You've been sighing and cursing under your breath all day." Haru tilts his head in my direction. He's standing at the counter beside me where he seasons a large metal bowl of boiled spinach, mixing it with plastic-gloved hands. His voice is soft enough that anyone in the adjoining living area of our dorm can't hear. "We don't have to talk about it." He shrugs.

I grunt, considering whether to tell him. He will probably keep the situation a secret. "The new stylist," I finally say.

"Sky? What about her?" Haru asks.

"She overheard me asking Stylist Goh to have a different

stylist. She's angry with me, and I deserve it." I stir the pork in the pan with more force than necessary.

Haru hums under his breath. "It sounds like you should apologize, hyung."

At that moment, Jaesung strolls into the kitchen. "Is the food almost ready?" he asks hopefully, peering over Haru's shoulder.

Haru laughs. "Almost."

"Get out of the kitchen if you want it to be done faster," I say, but Haru's right. The only thing I can do is apologize to Sky. I just need to find the right time to do it, when I can speak to her alone.

FOUR

"In the deep darkness / You shine like a flaming red sun"

— "Red Moon," KARD

SKY

THE WEEK of shooting the MV and doing the album photoshoot are controlled chaos, the long days wearing me down. Between the frantic activity and hours of waiting to be needed while on set, I crash into bed every night and sleep dreamlessly. But seeing how good the members of KOSMIC look in their full ensemble in front of the cameras is worth it. Especially Byunho's outfits that I worked on.

I've barely had to interact with him since that day, since I've been avoiding him as much as possible.

Carpooling in a van from the office in Gangnam, the other stylists and I head to the set early on Friday morning. There are seven of us today — my supervisor, Ms. Goh, the three hair and makeup artists, Eunjung, the other assistant stylist, and Ms.

Goh's daughter, who's only a few years younger than me, about 20 years old.

The girl, Miyoung, is quiet and unexpressive, responding in short sentences to any comments addressed to her by the older ladies. What I gather from the conversation is that she's interested in being a stylist like her mom, and Ms. Goh let her tag along with us today.

Miyoung and I are given the task to unload the van together, which we do mostly in silence at first.

Maybe she could be a friend. I try to make a little bit of conversation in Korean.

"Are you in school to become a stylist?"

She doesn't meet my eyes, but she responds after a short pause in her quiet, breathy voice. "I finished school, but it's hard to find work."

I nod sympathetically. "It is. You need experience to find work, but you can't get experience if you're not hired. Do you like helping your mom?" I ask.

"I really like when Mom lets me come to the office with her after work."

We grab the last bins of supplies and close the back of the van. As we do, another van pulls into the lot, and Miyoung stops and stares in that direction.

It's the band and their manager.

Across the lot, I watch the guys climbing sleepily out of their van. I stifle a grin when I glimpse Simon in flannel pajamas and Jaesung with a messy bedhead, bleached blond hair sticking up in all directions like a baby bird. Tai, one of the only alert members of the group, nods at me and the other stylists as we head into the same warehouse we shot at several days before.

Once inside the stylist area contained by temporary walls, I set the bin of supplies I'm carrying on a table.

Miyoung slinks into a corner of the tent to watch her mother work.

I run to grab my breakfast out of my bag, and go to meet Changmin as he enters the tent. I've managed to switch with Eunjung so I don't have to work with Byunho.

"Morning," Changmin says, rubbing his face as he sinks into a chair. I offer him one of the pastries I grabbed for breakfast this morning, but he shakes his head and pats his flat, muscled stomach with a chagrined smile. "Can't. Thanks though."

"Are you serious? You're so fit. A bite of something sweet won't hurt." I shake my head.

"Did you say sweet?" Jaesung asks, making me jump as his face appears, looking over my shoulder. His eyes are locked on the bag with the custard-filled bun inside.

My heart melts. "Here." I hand it over to him.

"Thank youuuu," he sings, sticking his nose in the bag and inhaling deeply. "I think I love you."

"Me or the food?" I tease.

Jaesung glances up, a mischievous grin crossing his face. "You." KOSMIC's maknae winks at me, then strolls off with his prize.

I shake my head with a little laugh, flustered. "Sorry, was I not supposed to give it to him?" I ask, turning back to Changmin, who chuckles and waves a hand in response to my question.

"Jaesung's a bottomless pit. He can eat anything and not gain weight."

Unlike Byunho, working with Changmin doesn't make my skin prickle with self-consciousness. Even though he's beautiful, like a prince from a fairy tale, there's something very reassuring about Changmin's presence. I can't help but be comfortable with him.

I'm a bit concerned at how hard Changmin is being on

himself. "I mean, it probably wouldn't hurt any of you to gain a few pounds."

"It's okay. We eat a lot when it's not comeback season, and we ate really well last night because Byunho and Haru made dinner," Changmin reassures me. I blink, trying to picture Byunho cooking.

"Now that you've fed Jaesung, though, he probably won't leave you alone," Changmin warns.

I laugh. "I'm sure I can deal with it. Here, please put these on." I pass him his outfit.

"Thank you." Changmin gets up to go change. Today the guys are filming a dance scene in front of a green screen. This scene will show KOSMIC dancing the choreography on an asteroid flying through space. I'm not sure leather and ripped jeans are very realistic attire for space, but it looks cool.

"How do I look?" Changmin asks, coming out from behind the changing screen. He's wearing a black V-necked sleeveless shirt embroidered with tiny silver stars (which will be cinched at the waist with a leather corset that I still need to help him put on) paired with midnight blue pants dripping with chains. The outfit is Eunjung's design. He spreads his arms and does a slow spin. Then looks at me expectantly.

I roll my eyes and step closer to adjust his collar. "You know you look good."

He laughs, cheek dimpling as I look up at him. "I'm supposed to act like I don't know that."

As I step away, I catch movement from the corner of my eye. Byunho is watching us from across the tent with an unreadable expression in his dark eyes. I jerk my gaze away, feeling my face flush.

Then I look back, because he's wearing the top that I made.

My creation for this set is an asymmetrical fiery red top composed of strips of fabric stretched between metal rings of varied sizes, through which teasing glimpses of Byunho's bare torso are visible. This top is paired with shiny black leather pants and heeled boots. My fingers itch to help Eunjung as I watch her fasten the ties in the back. They're a little tricky.

"Everything okay?" Changmin asks me.

"Yeah, fine. Let's get this corset on you."

I cinch the corset at Changmin's waist, which emphasizes his narrow hips and waist in contrast to his broader shoulders. He sits back down in the makeup chair.

The makeup artist comes to do his hair and makeup, and I leave her to it and look for something else to do.

Simon is struggling nearby to put on a half-sleeve leather harness contraption over his tightly fitted top. I dash over. "Hey, let me help with that." Together we get the harness thing over his shoulder and the multiple buckles fastened.

"Thanks." The singer cocks his head as he gives me a slight smile, his blue contact lenses bright and startling. His hair is dyed a greenish-black for this comeback, and his cheekbones are sharp enough to cut glass. Along with Byunho and Tai, I always considered Simon to be one of the most intimidating members. His British accent is also extremely sexy and one of the reasons he's such a popular member. Almost as popular as Hajun was.

"You know, it's a good thing you're here. Miss Kim is smart to put an American on our styling team. Especially given all of the fashion-related scandals the K-Pop world has had," Simon says.

I nod, a little surprised by this astute assessment of my purpose on the team. "Yeah, she wants the company to have a more globally aware business strategy."

"It's definitely time." Simon gives me a slight smile. "Let me know if you ever need anything. It's hard coming to a new country."

"Oh, sure. Thank you." Simon, like me, was born and raised

in an English speaking country and if I remember correctly, didn't speak Korean well when he came here to train. My heart is warmed by his consideration.

I circle back to Changmin, whose makeup is now done.

The makeup artist put on silver eyeliner, adding subtle shadow and some glitter around his eyes, and stuck several tiny fake gems to one of his cheekbones.

"Wow. You look great," I say.

I swear the tips of Changmin's ears turn red. I'm about to tease him when Tai appears beside me, saying something to Changmin that I don't quite catch.

Tai is wearing a fishnet cropped top and the obligatory leather—his body is all chiseled muscle and I can't even look at the guy without getting an eyeful of abs or biceps that have been slathered with body oil.

Infinities are going to lose their minds when they see this music video.

"Time to go film," Changmin translates to English for me, getting up from the makeup chair and following Tai and the others. His ears are still red, but I don't think it was my compliment that did it.

I wonder what did.

"You'll do great!" I watch the members file out.

Jaesung shoots me a finger heart, and I return the gesture with a grin.

Then I go with the other stylists to watch from a safe distance as KOSMIC gets into position in front of the camera.

The music starts, the band explodes into simultaneous movement, like different limbs of the same organism. A couple minutes later, pyrotechnics go off, making me flinch—but the guys don't react at all.

During the fourth take, as the pyrotechnics go off again, I notice something off about Byunho's top. One of the pieces of fabric has come loose and is dangling from his shoulder. As I watch in helpless dread, it unravels further until the top is hanging halfway off him.

The director yells to stop the filming. Eunjung starts forward to fix the wardrobe malfunction, but Ms. Goh shakes her head and points at me. "You made it. You fix it," she tells me.

Burning with embarrassment, I grab up the clear plastic bag with all of the emergency pins and tape and head toward the guys, trying to ignore all of the eyes of the staff on me. My sneakers crunch on the gravel of the set, fake fog eddying around me and filling the air with its acrid odor.

Byunho walks toward me, meeting me at the rim of the fake crater. His eye makeup is smoky, enhancing the intensity of his dark gaze, now aimed at me.

BYUNHO

I climb up the side of the gravel hill to where Sky stands, clutching her tools and blinking the smoky sting of dry ice fog out of her eyes, stopping when I'm at eye level with her. She's standing just above me, only a few feet away. Here, the fog is so thick that we're partially obscured from the crew's view.

"Um," Sky starts, at the same time as I say in English, "I want to apologize."

We stare at each other.

"I'm the one who made the faulty costume," she says.

I shake my head. "No, about before... I was rude. I was embarrassed. I thought it would be easier for you not to work with me, since you feel awkward around me. I'm sorry." I bow in apology.

Sky gapes at me. "Wait, *you* were embarrassed?"

"Yes," I admit, trying not to scowl.

"Oh."

"We need to begin filming again soon!" calls the director.

"Can—"

"—Yeah, let me—"

I hold absolutely still as she steps close, close enough that I feel her breath on the sweat-damp skin of my neck while she puts the shirt back together. "I hope you will accept my apology," I say.

She looks up at me, her expression still a bit guarded. "I'll think about it."

SKY

I busy myself tying the top back together (tucking a few safety pins in key areas this time, to account for the energetic choreo) and trying to ignore the riot of butterflies in my stomach from touching Byunho's smooth golden skin.

"Done. You can go back to filming now." I don't think it would have fallen apart had I been the one to put it on him in the first place, which is on me.

"Thank you." One side of Byunho's mouth curves in a hesitant smile, making my heart stutter, before he turns and goes back on the set.

I can finally breathe again. Some people don't know how to apologize. The fact that he did means, maybe, that he's not as big of a jerk as I thought.

Either way, I don't know what to do about how he makes me feel when I'm around him.

AFTER THE SHOOT, I pack up with the rest of the stylists. Deciding to not let someone else handle my designs again, I take the top I designed for Byunho back from Stylist Eunjung.

I examine the top closely. The fasteners that hold the different parts of the top together are loose, attached only by a few strings of thread.

But this is the first time Byunho has worn it, so it shouldn't be falling apart. Weird.

I make a note to fix it before the comeback stages, and put it away.

FIVE

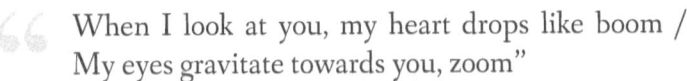 When I look at you, my heart drops like boom /
My eyes gravitate towards you, zoom"

— "Shoong!" Taeyang ft. Lisa

BYUNHO

THE NEXT MORNING is supposed to be the start of a short, several-day break before the music video's release and comeback shows, so I had planned to sleep in—but Tai is touching my shoulder and telling me to wake up long before I'm ready.

I groan, burying my face in my pillow. "What? It can't be noon already."

"Sangjin is here. Says he needs to talk with you. Sounds important." Sangjin is our band manager.

"Fuck." I sit up, rubbing the sleep from my eyes. Tai stands above me, hair wet from the shower and wearing a fresh t-shirt and pants. My roommate is an early bird who wakes up before everyone else to work out, even on our days off. I join him a lot, but he's the one who's fanatic about it. "Why?"

"I guess the company has a last minute promotion for you to do."

"Just me?"

"Just you." Tai shrugs apologetically. "There's coffee in the kitchen."

I sigh. "Tell him I'll be out in five minutes."

* * *

"SORRY TO WAKE you early on your day off, but an opportunity has come up. The National Tourism Organization wants you to shoot some promotion videos for them in Busan," Sangjin tells me as we sit in the dorm living room. I slouch on the couch, sipping my black coffee and longing to return to my bed.

"Why me?" I ask. We're in the middle of getting ready for our first comeback since the scandal. It's not exactly the best time.

"You're a member of one of the most popular K-Pop groups in the world, and Busan is your hometown. The government thinks a promotion stunt from you will drive tourism. You're one of a handful of idols they're hiring for this promotional campaign." Sangjin pauses, noticing my blank stare. "They've offered a generous sum of money."

I snort. Knowing the expectations listed in my contract, CKM has already informally accepted on my behalf. I can tell from the way Sangjin keeps wincing regretfully.

"Can't it wait until after the new album is released?"

"CKM management thinks it's better to do it now. There won't be enough time between schedules once the album drops. You'll only be gone for a few days, and you can catch up on practice when you come back."

And pull several days with little to no sleep—not that

management cares about that. I could refuse, but opportunities don't last forever. KOSMIC's popularity could fade. We might not even reunite after going to the military. Since Hajun left, that outcome looks more possible than ever. As much as I hate to admit it, I shouldn't skip an opportunity like this.

"Fine. But I better see extra zeros on my paycheck."

"You will." Sangjin lets out a breath, relieved, then digs in his briefcase and produces a stack of papers and a pen. "Here's the contract. Here's where it says how much you'll be paid." He taps the large number with his pen. "On the last page is your itinerary."

I flip through the papers on the coffee table, signing as I go. One thing you don't realize about being an idol is how much paperwork you have to sign.

Handing the promotional contract back to Sangjin, I scan the schedule. They want me to leave today and film tomorrow and the next day, doing tourist things around the city that was my home years ago.

"You can take your own car. While you're traveling, you should film a travel vlog on this camera I've brought for you for a behind-the-scenes video, and try to film other short clips during spare time. You know the drill." Sangjin produces a camera bag from his briefcase. "The hotel is reserved for you and the staff member we're sending with you, and you meet the tourism org camera crew in the morning. I don't know the details, but they'll handle the logistics. I'm sorry my schedule doesn't allow me to go with you."

I stand, rubbing the back of my neck with a sigh. "I guess I should go get packed, then."

SKY

A horrible, incessant noise wakes me up from a deep sleep. My phone is ringing.

I fumble, bleary-eyed, for the infernal device on my nightstand. My boss's name is on the screen. Why is she calling me on my day off?

"Yeoboseyo?" I answer, hoping that my sleepy brain can keep up with a conversation with her.

Mrs. Go's voice speaks into my ear, in English. "You need to work this weekend."

I fight a yawn.

Wait, what?

"We"—meaning herself and the other staff on the styling team—"are too busy preparing the comeback and you must go on a business trip to Busan."

I didn't sign up for random weekend business trips. At least, I don't think I did. "All of a sudden? What's the reason?" I pull up a mental map of South Korea. Busan is a big city on the southern coast, the opposite side of the country.

"It's a promotional activity sponsored by the government's tourism organization. You'll go with one of the members of KOSMIC and work as his personal stylist, making sure he looks good for the cameras. You'll be sent funds for personal spending."

"Wait, who is it?" My heart lurches with a strange mixture of dread and excitement, as if I already know the answer.

"Seo Byunho. He's on his way to pick you up soon, so you should get ready."

Oh no.

"You gave him my *address*?" I glance out my window, as if Byunho might already be standing out on the street.

"You need to leave as soon as possible. He'll be there at 10 A.M."

I check the clock. It's already 9:02! That leaves me less than an hour to get ready.

I scramble out of my tangled bedsheets, almost face-planting on the floor, while Ms. Goh explains I'll be staying at a hotel with Byunho for three nights (separate rooms, obviously) and spending all day with him for four days straight.

The universe must be laughing at me.

SIX

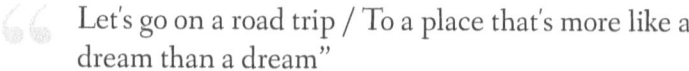 Let's go on a road trip / To a place that's more like a dream than a dream"

— "Road Trip," NCT 127

BYUNHO

THE STAFF MEMBER they chose to send with me is Sky. When Sangjin told me, I wanted to kick myself. The next few days are sure to be... interesting. Especially because I'm not sure Sky is ready to accept my apology for what happened.

I pull onto the narrow one-way street outside of her address and glance up at what must be her apartment building—a few residential floors set above a couple storefronts at street level. Because I don't have her KakaoTalk and can't bring myself to call her actual number Sangjin gave me yet, I just put the car in park and wait.

Sky comes through the door with a full backpack and huge suitcase, struggling a bit with the door. I pop the trunk as I get out of the car—pulling my face mask up over my nose so that passerby won't recognize me— and meet her halfway across the street.

"Oh, I got it, it's fine!" she says, but I take the suitcase from her anyway. It's surprisingly heavy, and I wonder what she could possibly have in there. I put the bag in the trunk beside my duffel bag. Then, I open the door on the passenger side before she can do it herself.

Brows raised in surprise, she gives me an awkward smile as I hold the door. "Thanks." Hesitating briefly, she slides into my car.

Closing the door behind her, I take a deep breath before I get in on my side.

SKY

Byunho owns a Lamborghini, because of course he does. That's the only explanation for the sports car that just pulled up outside my apartment.

I barely had enough time to make myself presentable after throwing everything I might need into my suitcase. Grabbing my bags, I head outside.

To my surprise, Byunho comes over and takes the heaviest bag from me without even a greeting. I protest, but in typical Byunho fashion, he ignores me. I follow him to his car, where he holds the passenger door for me. Giving him a shy smile when we make eye contact, I quickly get in the car, realizing my heart is pounding and my palms are sweating.

It's just a road trip with someone whose fancams I used to watch religiously. Who confuses the hell out of me now that I know him in real life. No big deal.

Byunho folds his body into the driver's seat and waits for a pedestrian to cross the street before pulling away from the curb. He wears his long hair tied back in a ponytail.

My phone dings with a text.

It's from Aera:

> Hey. I just got the news you're going to Busan with Byunho. I'm sorry they sprang this on you. If you want to say no, I'll back you up.

> You're a little late. I'm already in the car with him!

I sneak a peek at the man out of the corner of my eye. He's concentrating on the road, navigating with practiced ease and calm through Seoul traffic, seeming not at all bothered by the fact that we haven't yet said a proper sentence to one another. Some R&B music plays at low volume on the speakers. This is the fanciest car I've ever ridden in.

I have no idea where Byunho and I stand. All of our interactions have been confusing for me, to say the least. I try to keep hold of my anxiety about being in such close proximity with him by watching the passing scenery outside the car windows–buildings and cars, trees and sky.

BYUNHO

"What do you think of Korea?" I ask in English, if only to break the silence.

Sky was worrying her bottom lip with her teeth and clutching her hands together in her lap as she stared out the window.

Now she seems to remember someone else is in the car with her. I almost regret disturbing whatever was going on inside her head, but the car has just entered a long tunnel, and the sudden lack of sunlight makes the space inside the car closer, darker. I feel emboldened to ask about her. And she's not going to speak to me unless I make her.

"Oh. I like it," she says.

"But?" I prompt. She has to have other thoughts about it.

"Well, I haven't been able to explore very much. I've been to cafes around Seoul, and I love that, but I haven't done much else. Work consumes a lot of my time...but well, I guess you know what that's like." Sky trails off, laughing in embarrassment.

I chuckle. "Yes. But you're about to see some more of Korea." We've just emerged from the tunnel, and I lift my hand off the wheel to gesture to the scenery.

"What is Busan like?"

After leaving years ago, I've both missed it more than I can admit and felt burdened whenever I go home. "It's the most beautiful city in the world," I say. In my opinion, it still is.

"How long has it been since you went back?"

I consider her question. "More than a year. I visit my mother and her family when I can." Although that's not very often. "Tell me about you. If you're really my fan, then you already know about me."

She coughs in embarrassment, which makes my lips curve. "It's not like I know that much," she says defensively. Which is true. Fans only know what we want them to know. After a pause, she asks, with a bit of shyness in her voice, "What do you want to know about me?"

SKY

"Where are you from? What is your family like?" Byunho asks, his voice casual and yet, I get the feeling that nothing Byunho does is ever without intent.

I shift in my seat, feeling overwhelmed to have his attention focused on me this way.

"I'm from Massachusetts. It's kind of close to New York." The U.S. is big and actually, I wouldn't expect someone who's not from the U.S. to know where Massachusetts is. "And my parents are the best. They're lawyers. They met in college and still love each other so much, it's kind of gross. They really wanted me to follow in their footsteps, but I wanted something different." I shrug, even though Byunho's watching the road and not me. "After graduating fashion design school, I did a temporary internship in New York City. While I was looking for a full-time position, the stylist opening at CKM happened. So now I'm in Korea doing fashion stuff. But I have a little brother who's in high school, Tony, and he doesn't want to be a lawyer either. So I guess they're out of luck." I stop, feeling self-conscious about talking so much.

"They seem lucky to me," Byunho replies, and after a pause adds, "For you to be their daughter, I mean."

My cheeks heat. "You're just saying that to make me like you again."

Byunho chuckles and shoots a glance in my direction. "Is it working?"

My heart skips a beat. I'm saved from having to answer when my phone rings. Aera's name pops up on the screen.

"Oh, um. Do you mind?" I ask Byunho, my finger hovering over the answer button.

He shakes his head, eyes on the road, so I swipe and put the phone up to my ear. "Hey. Is everything okay?" she asks me.

"Yeah," I reply. "We're on our way to Busan now." We've finally made it out of Seoul itself, taller buildings dropping away to a highway lined by trees, mountains in the distance.

"Okay. If you need anything at all, let me know. No-notice assignments like this are against company policy, so I will be talking with your supervisor about this." Aera takes her role as Chief Operations Officer of CKM Entertainment very seriously. It's still hard to reconcile her public identity with the soft-hearted personality that lies beneath her shell. "And if Byunho tries anything with you, he can kiss his contract with the company goodbye."

I wince, hoping that Byunho didn't hear that. "Okay, *Mom*. See you when I get back."

"Don't call me that. But yes, coffee on me when you get back," she promises. "Be safe and don't hesitate to contact me." Aera hangs up, already on to the next item in her busy schedule.

An awkward silence descends on the car once again. I remember Aera mentioning that Byunho and Tai were the two members of KOSMIC who were most furious when Hajun was forced to leave the band, and that they still haven't spoken to her since then.

I lean my head against the cool glass of the window.

BYUNHO

I pretend not to hear Kim Aera's voice threatening to get me fired if I "try anything" with Sky.

After a period of silence, I glance over to find that Sky has fallen asleep. Her eyes are closed, and her dark curls have fallen across the smooth skin of her cheek, her chest rising and falling steadily with her breathing.

There's no denying that I find her attractive, that I was attracted to her the moment I saw her at the hotel in New York a year ago—I haven't been able to admit that to myself until now. That is one of the reasons that I didn't want to work with her. Now we have no choice but to spend the next several days together, but I can't let myself be attracted to her.

Not only is she friends with Kim Aera, but she's a staff member, and a fan. Those are enough reasons to keep her at arm's length.

And yet, I can't help but want to know more about her. Despite myself, I want her to like me.

I continue on the highway across the country, back to the city where I was born.

SKY

I must have fallen asleep at some point, because it takes me a moment to remember where I am: in the car with an international superstar. I jolt upright, hoping that I didn't snore, or drool on his fancy leather car seat. What's worse, I immediately recognize the pressure in my bladder telling me that I desperately have to pee.

"We're almost there," Byunho says. Which means I must have slept for several hours.

"Sorry," I say, wincing and patting my hair down, hoping I don't have bedhead. "Um, could we pull over somewhere? I need to use the restroom."

"No problem." Byunho takes the next exit ramp and pulls into a gas station. He nods at the glove box. "Could you get the hat and glasses for me?"

I retrieve the items—a SUPREME beanie and a pair of Louis Vouitton sunglasses—and pass them to him, trying to ignore the warm brush of his fingers against mine as he takes them. Byunho puts them on along with a black face mask, obscuring his identity from the casual observer, before stepping out of the car to fuel it. I hop out and run into the gas station.

When I come out of the gas station, Byunho leans against his car and watches me cross the lot, as if making sure I make it back to the car. We pull out of the gas station and get back on the road.

"If you want to keep a low profile, isn't a Lamborghini a bit conspicuous?" I ask him.

I think I see him hold back a smirk. "I don't know what you're talking about."

Soon the Busan skyline comes into view, skyscrapers reaching for the blue sky. The afternoon traffic slows us to a crawl, then a stop.

Byunho sighs and taps his fingers on the wheel. "Could you do something for me?" he asks suddenly.

I sit up straighter. "What?"

"Do you think you could film me with the camera under your seat? I'm supposed to be vlogging some behind the scenes for this trip."

"Sure." I reach under the seat and pull out a camera case. After a few minutes of figuring out how it works, I turn on the video and point it at Byunho.

He flashes a practiced smile at the camera (different from his real lopsided smile, I note), instantly switching into idol mode. "Hi Infinities," he says in Korean. While pointing the camera at him, I concentrate hard to understand everything he's saying at the speed with which he's saying it. "I'm in my car now, going to Busan to film a special promotion for my hometown. I'm excited to show Infinities the beautiful places in Busan. We're about to have a comeback as well, so I hope you'll love it. I worked hard on writing songs on the album, and I can't wait for you to hear them." It's surreal to be on the other side of the camera, being here for the filming of a video that other fans will watch on YouTube.

Byunho nods at me that I can stop the video. I do and by then, the traffic is moving forward again.

BYUNHO

We arrive at the hotel and head inside to check in at the front desk, leaving my car briefly in the care of the valet. The hotel is nice, but small, with a sleek modern interior in a slate-gray color palette.

"We can take your bags to your room," the clerk says, his eyes shifting between me and Sky, lingering on Sky with a curiosity that I don't like.

I raise a brow at him. "Please do."

We return to my car. It's only mid-afternoon, and both of us are hungry and have nothing to do until tomorrow morning. "Where are we going now?" Sky asks.

There's one place that I need to go. "Home."

SEVEN

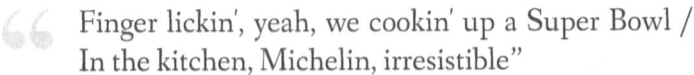 Finger lickin', yeah, we cookin' up a Super Bowl /
In the kitchen, Michelin, irresistible"

— "Super Bowl," Stray Kids

SKY

BYUNHO'S FAMILY home is apparently a fried chicken restaurant.

The door bell dings as we walk inside. My nerves make me jump at the sound. Meeting Byunho's parents isn't something I'm exactly prepared to do, but Byunho didn't even give me the option to stay behind at the hotel, and somehow I'm here now.

There are several customers at the tables, and a middle-aged woman in an apron comes out of the kitchen with a couple baskets of fried chicken. I have to admit that it smells good, even though I stopped eating meat in high school.

The woman does a double-take at us as she sets the baskets down. "Son?" she gasps, eyes wide.

"I'm home, Eomoni," Byunho says.

Byunho's mother charges toward us and barely stops herself from throwing her arms around Byunho when she realizes she has grease on her apron. She settles for patting his arms and face instead, as if checking to see that he's alright. "Omo, you look so skinny. You're not eating enough. But what are you doing here?"

I stand there awkwardly as Byunho's mother fusses over him. He puts up with it without complaint, which is uncharacteristic of what I know about him. "I'm here for a short promotional shoot over the next couple of days." His voice and pronunciation are different speaking in the Busan satoori dialect, which makes it harder to understand what he's saying. "This is Sky, she works with me at the company as a stylist."

Byunho's mother turns and blinks at me, then smiles and bows. "I'm Hyunok," she says in Korean, then hesitates. "Can she speak Korean?" she asks her son.

"I can speak a little bit, ajumeoni," I say with a bow, self-conscious from Hyunok's attention. "I'm still learning."

"Wow, you speak it so well." She's just being kind, but I thank her anyway. "Welcome to my restaurant. Byunho, you should make her something to eat. I don't have time to feed you both." She gives him a pointed look, smiles at me, and bustles off.

I laugh in embarrassment, regretting being here because I'll have to refuse any fried chicken that I'm offered. Which is too bad, because I'm starving. "That's okay, you don't need to make me food. I actually don't eat meat..."

Byunho considers. "That's fine. I can make our fried chicken recipe with tofu."

He heads toward the back. I want to tell him not to worry about it, but instead of shouting it across the restaurant, I hurry after him. The restaurant's few other patrons watch with curiosity. Byunho is talking with Hyunok when I go through the door into the kitchen. Hyunok shrugs and waves him off.

"You don't have to do that," I tell Byunho, walking up beside him as he pulls on an apron. He's taken off his mask.

Byunho snorts, a slight smirk tilting his mouth up. "Actually, I'm kind of hungry. So I'm not just doing it for you. But if you want to help, you can."

At the kitchen sink, he rolls up his sleeves to the elbow and lathers his hands with soap. I try not to stare at the veins in his forearms.

"Okay," I say. Helping him is preferable to standing around awkwardly. "Just tell me what to do."

I wash my hands in the sink as Byunho gets tofu and some other ingredients out of the fridge and whips up a batter. He instructs me to tear the blocks of tofu into chunks and drop them in the bowl of batter, coating them. Using chopsticks, we then roll the batter-covered tofu in flour.

Byunho then takes the bowl of tofu and starts frying them in hot oil, while I chop up some garlic and scallions. The practiced ease with which he moves around in the kitchen is somehow so attractive. My face heats as he comes up to stand right beside me, although he's just taking the garlic and scallions I chopped.

He puts the garlic in a pan and adds a red paste and vinegar, making a sauce. When the tofu is done frying, he adds the tofu to the pan with the sauce and stirs it in, frying it a bit longer. The smell makes my stomach growl and my mouth water, realizing just how hungry I am from not eating all day. He takes the tofu out of the pan and puts it on a large plate, to which I add the chopped scallion and some sesame seeds.

"I hope you like spicy," Byunho says as we take the plate out into the restaurant, sitting down at a table to eat.

"I like spicy," I reply, not sure why I'm blushing. "Thanks for the food." The fact that he would go out of his way to make a vegetarian fried "chicken" for me is so weirdly kind of him that I wonder if he's the same Byunho who asked my supervisor not to work with me only a couple weeks ago.

We dig in and demolish the plate of food. It's delicious and completely satisfying.

By now the dinner rush has started, and people are starting to notice Byunho. A group of teenage girls are staring at him with wide eyes. One of them tries to discreetly point her phone at us. Byunho puts his mask back on and stands. "Follow me."

We go back through the kitchen, where Hyunok is busy cooking up orders. "We're going upstairs."

She waves us away and we go through a door and up a set of stairs that lead into an apartment. I follow Byunho's lead in taking off my shoes by the door. As I gaze around the smallish living room, he goes into the apartment's kitchen. "Want a drink?" he asks, looking over at me.

"Water?" My eyes have caught on a framed photo on the wall of Hyunok beside a man who must be Byunho's dad, and a teenage Byunho holding a toddler-aged girl, all standing together at the front of the restaurant downstairs. Everyone in the photo wears a serious expression except for the toddler with her gap-toothed smile. I notice the little girl is holding the blue elephant plushie that Byunho had that first day I met him in New York. Suddenly, it all makes sense.

Byunho brings a water to where I'm still standing in front of the photo. "Is that your little sister?" I ask him.

"Yeah, Hyunjoo. She should be getting home from her study group soon."

I nod and take a drink of water. "She gave you that elephant, didn't she?" I point at the photo.

Byunho laughs and looks at the ceiling, embarrassed. "Oh, that. She gave it to me for good luck when I left to be a trainee. I never told the members why I have it, so they just made fun of me for it." He shrugs.

My heart aches at how sweet that is. "So you grew up here?"

"More or less."

"It must be nice to be home. Thanks for sharing it with me."

Byunho looks away from me again, and I worry I've made things awkward by being here. But I don't have long to worry about it, as the front door opens and a teenage girl rushes into the apartment wearing a huge smile, kicking off her shoes and dropping her backpack carelessly on the ground. "Oppa! I heard you were home!"

Hyunjoo flings herself at Byunho, wrapping her arms around his waist. He's grinning widely as he hugs her back with one arm, messing up her dark hair with his other hand. "You got taller," he says teasingly, though she only barely comes up to his shoulder.

"Well, your hair is red—are you a tomato?" She struggles free and smoothes her hair down. They have the same thick, expressive brows.

Noticing me, she looks questioningly at Byunho. "Who's that?"

"I'm Sky. I work with your brother as a stylist," I say in Korean.

She bows and smiles shyly. "Are you from America?" she asks in English.

"Yes. Kind of near New York." Her curiosity is sweet.

"She went to Harvard," Byunho says. I try to remember when I told Byunho this and realize that I didn't. I'm surprised he remembered such a detail about me. Even though I didn't graduate.

Hyunjoo's eyes light up with wonder. "Wow, really? I'm studying English really hard so hopefully I can go to school in

America. I graduate in only a few years. I don't think I would get into such a great school."

"Whatever school you go to and whatever you decide to do, you'll do amazing." I give her a reassuring smile.

The front door opens again, and I see Byunho tense. The man from the photo comes into view, wearing a suit and carrying a briefcase. "Hyunok told me you were here," he says.

"Abeoji." The joy is gone from Byunho's face, replaced by a stony lack of emotion. "I'm in town for a few days, so I just wanted to say hello to Eomoni and Hyunjoo."

I'm not imagining the tenseness in the room.

"We were just leaving," Byunho says, and Hyunjoo makes a protesting sound before silencing herself.

Byunho's father says nothing, barely taking notice of me as Byunho and Hyunjoo hug goodbye. We put our shoes on, and leave the apartment.

"Leaving so soon?" Hyunok asks down in the restaurant's kitchen, her eyes holding a sad desperation. But Byunho just hugs her goodbye, and we leave.

BYUNHO

As I drive us back to the hotel, I can feel the questions Sky is trying not to ask in the weighted silence between us. "You can ask," I mutter with a sigh.

"It's okay. You don't need to tell me anything you don't want to about your dad," she says after a pause.

"He's not my father," I correct her. "He married my mom and they had Hyunjoo when I was a kid."

"Oh. So... you don't get along?"

I chuckle humorlessly. "Not really."

"I'm sorry." She's twisting her hands together in her lap, as if worried she's upset me.

I shrug it off. "It's in the past." I don't want to think about it anymore, not when I could be getting to know Sky better. The gentle way she interacted with Hyunjoo, I can almost picture her with her own younger sibling.

And I can appreciate how much she seemed to enjoy the food I cooked for her, the way her eyes widened in pleasure as she took the first bite. I may not have ever wanted to get into the family business of running a restaurant, but I still feel satisfied by my ability to please Sky with my cooking.

I'm not sure I want to think too much about why that is.

EIGHT

It's getting out of control / This fire is spreading too fast"

— "Playing with Fire," BLACKPINK

SKY

BACK AT THE HOTEL, we take the elevator up to our rooms. Although all we did today was travel and meet Byunho's family, I'm exhausted.

My key card sleeve has my room number on it. Byunho and I walk down the hallway, expecting to have two rooms next to each other. But Byunho and I stop in front of the same door.

"Let me see that," he says, and I show him the number on my key card's sleeve. It's the same as his, Room 37.

"They must have accidentally given one of us the wrong card?" I ask. But when we go inside the room, both of our suitcases are there at the foot of the two double beds.

"Maybe they just accidentally booked one room instead of two," I guess, panicking internally. The rooms were reserved by the organization sponsoring Byunho—all we had to do earlier was confirm Byunho's name and pick up the room keys. But this is a disaster.

"I'll go talk to the front desk," Byunho mutters. "You can have this room."

"You sure?" I ask doubtfully. Because of the comeback, he's been working 10-15 hour days for the past couple weeks. Now that I'm looking, I can tell how tired he is—his broad shoulders are slightly curved, and there are shadows beneath his eyes.

He nods and brushes past me to the door, leaving me alone.

It's only around 7 p.m., but I decide to get ready for bed—washing my face, brushing my teeth, and changing into an oversized t-shirt and some gym shorts.

I watch the sun begin to set, a slice of hazy orange over the shimmering blue sea I can see between neighboring buildings.

BYUNHO

"We're sorry, but your sponsor only paid for one room," says the desk clerk, a different man from the one who checked us in earlier today.

"Then let me pay for another one myself."

The clerk taps around on the keyboard for a couple minutes, while I wait in silence, impatient. "I'm afraid all of the rooms are reserved or unavailable for late booking," he says, not sounding very sorry at all.

I nearly growl in frustration. "Fine." I cross the lobby and take the elevator back upstairs. I'll just have to call other hotels and book a room.

Knocking on the door to Room 37, I wait for Sky to let me in even though I have my key. She opens the door a moment later wearing only a long shirt and shorts, revealing a glimpse of her long, smooth brown legs.

"Any luck?" she asks, crossing her arms over her chest.

"No," I answer after a beat, stepping into the room and shutting the door behind me. I turn back to Sky, keeping my eyes on her face. "The hotel doesn't have any available rooms. I'll have to go somewhere else."

"I'm sure this is all just a mistake." Sky frowns, and I watch her emotions flicker across her face—hesitation, then decision. "We're both tired. Let's both sleep here, just for tonight," she suggests. "We'll get it all sorted out tomorrow."

She's washed her makeup off, which has the effect of softening her features. I can't help but think I prefer her this way. A dangerous thought.

"It's okay. I really don't mind," she continues, seeming to take my silence for hesitation. "We can respect each other's personal space. It's not a big deal."

It might not be a big deal to her, with all her American casualness. But she doesn't know the things that seeing her like this—sitting on a bed, with her loose curls framing her face—makes me feel.

Despite a voice in my head yelling that this is a terrible idea, my exhaustion from weeks of comeback preparation forces me to agree. I nod wearily. "Just for tonight."

SKY

Byunho wastes no time checking the entire room for hidden cameras—in lamps, vents, and other places I wouldn't even think of. While normally I would find this paranoid behavior, I guess as an idol he's right to be cautious.

Once he's satisfied that there are no hidden cameras in the room, he shuts himself in the bathroom to shower. He's barely looked at or spoken with me, and I wonder if the idea of sharing a room with me is really so horrible to him.

Pulling on a satin hair bonnet over my curls, I tuck myself into the bed closer to the window and check my phone.

Aera texted me.

> Did you make it to Busan safe?

> Yep! Don't worry

I chew on my thumbnail, worrying about myself. It's starting to hit me that I'm sharing a hotel room with Byunho Seo, a man who I've had a celebrity crush on for years.

Is this even allowed? What will happen if the company finds out? How the hell am I supposed to be professional in a situation like this?

When the door to the bathroom opens, I'm so on edge that I jump. Byunho wears sweatpants and a loose tank top. He pulls a towel off his head, causing strands of his dark red, still-wet hair to stick to his neck and collarbones. His eyes catch mine, and I glance away quickly.

I pretend to stare at my phone as he folds his long body into the other bed mere feet away from my bed and clicks off his lamp. "Goodnight!" I chirp, reaching over to shut off my lamp as well, plunging the room into darkness.

"Goodnight," he replies a moment later, the deep rasp of his voice doing nothing to ease the tension in me.

I stare up toward the dark ceiling and try to breathe, my heart thundering in my chest. After what feels like forever, I calm my racing pulse and close my eyes. But despite the cloudlike softness of the mattress, I can't get comfortable. I feel feverish, too warm despite the air conditioner running on high. I lay on one side, then the other. I'm exhausted, but I can't sleep. Not with him so close.

It takes me hours before I finally slip into unconsciousness.

NINE

> The Busan beach there / Say la la la la la / Under
> the blue sky, this skyline"
>
> — "Ma City," BTS

BYUNHO

THE NEXT MORNING when my alarm wakes me, I haul
myself out of bed and get dressed in the bathroom. Sky is still
sleeping when I come out, the comforter kicked off and her arms
and legs wrapped around one of the pillows. Her mouth is open
and there's a little bit of drool at the corner of her lips.

She doesn't wake up when I speak to her with a raised voice.
I consider for a moment, then decide to wake her like I would
one of the members—by tossing a pillow at her, so I don't have to
touch her without her permission. Though I do it much more
gently than I would with one of the guys. The pillow hits her
squarely in the back, and she wakes instantly.

She lifts her head, looking around in confusion. "What the
hell?" she whines, wiping her mouth with the back of her hand

and sitting up. I try not to notice the way her shorts have ridden up around her thighs. "I was sleeping."

"We need to meet the sponsors at a cafe in an hour," I say.

"Oh, shit!"

SKY

Still grumbling over being woken by Byunho hitting me with a pillow, I start getting ready. The bags under my eyes are a testament to how poorly I slept, but I've got to do my job.

I dress in a pair of white pants and a black sleeveless top, with a pair of white flats, going for simple and professional while accounting for the rather warm weather. I make my face and hair presentable. When I exit the bathroom, I take a long look at Byunho, who's standing by the window looking out.

What he's wearing actually needs no changes—a pair of ripped jean shorts, white sneakers, and a black baggy t-shirt with a frowny face printed on it (how fitting). Out of all of the KOSMIC members, I've always admired his fashion sense. Today, it seems like we accidentally coordinated with both of us wearing black and white.

"Let me do your makeup," I say after a minute.

"Really?" he asks, turning and making a face that conveys he would rather not.

"It's my job. Come on."

BYUNHO

Sky directs me to sit down in the desk chair. She steps close, holding a makeup bag. Her perfume has a fruity, peach-like scent.

I hold still as she applies foundation to my face and blends it in, then takes an eyeliner pencil and carefully starts lining my eyes. I'm used to having this done to my face at this point, but there's something about having her standing between my knees with her face inches from my own that makes me feel a little crazy. Something possesses me to stare directly into her eyes, just to see what will happen. Her eyes meet mine, and slowly I smirk.

Her reaction is to pause what she's doing and bite her lip.

"What is it?" I ask, not so innocently.

"N-nothing!" she says quickly, flustered. I feel a flash of guilt for teasing her. She finishes blending shadow around my eyes and steps back to survey her work. "Okay, you're done."

We go down to the street, and walk a couple blocks to the cafe where we're to meet the representatives from the Tourism Organization. I order an iced black coffee, while Sky takes five minutes to decide what she's going to try, before ordering an iced vanilla dalgona coffee.

"I can't believe you just drink black coffee," she says combatively, in response to my raised brow. "There are so many drinks, why would you get the same thing every time?"

I shrug, amused. "Caffeine is caffeine."

"Unbelievable." She shakes her head in disgust. I take a seat at an empty table near the back while she waits for her drink.

By that time, the sponsors are here—a man and a woman wearing suits, who introduce themselves to me as Wang Daejung and Chun Yeojin, representatives of the Tourism Organization's publicity department in Busan.

Yeojin is a director and photographer herself. "We're so pleased to have you here," says Yeojin.

"Footage of such an internationally popular idol enjoying his hometown's popular attractions will surely boost Busan's tourism," Daejung adds.

Sky walks up to our table, holding her drink and looking a

little uncertain of herself. Both of the sponsors stare at her with confusion.

"This is my stylist, Sky Flores," I say.

Yeojin recovers first. "Oh, of course," she says in English. "Please, sit."

"Thank you," Sky says, sitting down beside me. Our chairs are close enough that her leg brushes mine beneath the table. I carefully stop myself from looking at her to check her reaction.

"I hope your accommodations have been pleasant, and that you will let us know if there is anything else you need," Daejung says.

"Actually, there is something. There was only one hotel room booked for us. Which as you can see, doesn't accommodate for the fact that we can't share a room." I let my expression show how unimpressed I am.

Daejung smiles nervously. "We were under the impression that CKM would be sending a male staff member with you. We'll have that sorted out by tonight," Daejung promises.

Then Yeojin gives a cheery smile. "Now, on to business. Today we'll be touring the eastern side of the city. Tomorrow we will start early to tour the western side and end at sunset. I know these places will all be familiar to you, but think of it as a vacation and be natural. I will personally be documenting all of it." She pats a pouch at her side which must contain her camera. "Shall we get started?"

SKY

The first stop is Haedong Yonggungsa Temple, a Buddhist temple perched on rocky cliffs beside the ocean.

Byunho turns on what I'm beginning to recognize as his "idol mode," as he describes coming to the temple as a child with his father to the camera. Yeojin eats it up, following Byunho around and getting shots of him everywhere in the temple, praising him almost excessively whenever she gets a particularly good clip. I hang back and trail behind them.

After climbing what seems like a million stairs, we leave the temple and get a late lunch at the food market right outside.

The skewered rice and deep-fried fish cakes melt in my mouth. We take a brief break from filming to eat while Yeojin checks her footage, leaving Byunho and I alone for a moment.

"I thought you didn't eat meat," Byunho remarks as I take another huge bite of fish cake.

"Oh, I still eat seafood. I'm a pescatarian, not pure vegetarian," I explain when my mouth is no longer too full to respond.

"Why?" he asks, curiosity in his voice.

I pause to get my thoughts in order. "I just like animals, so I try not to eat meat. Fish... I don't feel as bad about eating," I admit with a laugh. He smiles. "Is that story about coming to the temple with your dad true?"

"Why wouldn't it be true?" he asks, cocking a brow.

I raise my brows back at him.

"Yes, actually," he replies with a chuckle, then becomes serious again. He hesitates before admitting, "My father was raised Buddhist. He also didn't eat meat." His mouth quirks. "It's said that if you make a wish for your heart's desire at that temple, it will come true."

"What did you wish for?" I ask.

He gives me his lopsided smile. "To make music and become famous. It's not exactly what I thought it would be like, though."

"I know what you mean." I sigh, thinking about how nothing in the fashion world matches the idealism with which I envisioned it as a kid.

Before we can continue our discussion, Yeojin swoops in to usher us along to the next destination.

* * *

I QUICKLY REALIZE that wearing business flats was a bad idea when we reach Haeundae Beach.

My shoes fill with sand as I struggle to follow Yeojin and Byunho, who both have more reasonable footwear. The day is beautiful and cloudless, but way too hot. I sweat while trying to keep up with both of them.

Byunho stops by the rolling waves to take off his sneakers, then his shirt. My eyes widen, but I can't look away.

His body is lean, his muscles visible but not overly prominent. I notice for the first time the tattoo of KOSMIC's star-shaped logo that he has tattooed, just above his hipbone, in bluish-black ink.

My heart beats quickly even though what he's doing has nothing to do with me. He strips off his ripped jeans, revealing swim shorts beneath, and takes a quick dip in the water, which Yeojin films with an extra enthusiasm that is starting to annoy the crap out of me.

By now there is already a handful of people gathered watching, some of them taking photos and filming. "That's him!" I hear a young woman nearby whisper to her friend, as they giggle together behind their phones. "Why is he here?"

At least they're watching from a respectful distance, I guess. This isn't the only place that we've been noticed, or even followed, but nothing weird has happened yet, at least.

Maybe I'm one of them, an anonymous, insignificant girl with a delusional, one-sided celebrity crush. My stomach sinks with the realization that I'm not that different. I just have a job that gets me closer to See Byunho. I'm an imposter in this world.

As I stand on the beach with my heart in my throat, he looks over at me and sees me watching him. While holding my gaze, he steps out of the water. His body is a glistening gold beneath the sun, little droplets of water catching the light like diamonds, almost like the sunlight strikes him differently than other people. I can't breathe as he looks at me.

Yeojin intercepts him, pulling a small towel from her satchel for him to dry off with. He's no longer looking at me.

I turn away, lifting my hair off the sweaty back of my neck, tying it into a tighter bun.

* * *

I SIT in silence in the sky capsule ride, which is a small group capsule that moves on a rail along the coast. The views are stunning as the sun sets, and I choose to focus on that rather than Yeojin and Byunho having an interview for the camera, ignoring me.

I can't help but notice now that Yeojin is very beautiful—maybe Byunho likes her.

After the sun sets and night falls, we go to a seafood restaurant, which has a view of the lit-up Gwangan Bridge over the ocean, reflecting neon lights on the water. We sit by the window, and I can't help but think miserably about how this would be a perfect date night if I weren't here third-wheeling.

I don't like the jealous thoughts I'm having, but I can't help it. They converse rapidly in Korean, while I struggle to keep up. I give up and stuff myself with sashimi, scallops and prawns.

When Yeojin excuses herself to go to the bathroom, Byunho turns his attention to me. "Are you alright?" he asks, his eyes seeing more than I would like them to.

"Why wouldn't I be?" I say, but he stares at me until I give in. "Fine. It's stupid, but I feel like I'm following you both around on a date. She keeps flirting with you." *And you seem to like her more than me*, I don't add. I already sound absurdly jealous, which makes me dislike myself even more right now.

Byunho laughs at me, and my ego flinches. "I told you it was stupid," I mutter. I can't meet his eyes. I look down at the beach, the water shimmering with the reflection of the city lights.

"I'm not interested in her," Byunho says quietly, no longer laughing.

I look up. Something about the way he's looking at me, eyes dark and steady, makes my heart skip a beat.

"Alright!" Yeojin says loudly, coming back to the table with a big smile, completely oblivious. "I just got off the phone with Daejung, and he says he fixed your hotel situation. You are all set for tonight and each have your own rooms. I will call a cab."

We ride back to the hotel in tired silence, the moment that passed at dinner hanging unspoken between us. At the front desk, we pick up a new key card for the now-available room down the hall. Byunho gets his stuff from my room while I hover awkwardly.

"Night," I say as he opens the door. "See you in the morning."

He looks back at me and nods. I could almost swear he hesitates before closing the door.

Then I'm alone with my confusion and my delusions.

BYUNHO

What the hell am I doing? My reaction to Sky's jealousy was too unthinking. I practically admitted to Sky tonight that I'm interested in her. Despite my promises to myself, I'm failing miserably at keeping our relationship professional.

I don't care about Sky. I don't like her. Those are the

thoughts that I repeat in my mind as I fall asleep, but I know they ring hollow.

* * *

IN MY DREAM, *I'm on the beach and Sky is beside me. The beach is empty and the stars are shockingly clear and bright, swirling overhead like a time lapse film of the night sky.*

We look up at the stars together, and she brushes her fingers against my shoulder. I turn my head, and she tilts her face up to gaze into mine.

The look in her eyes startles me, and I question for a moment if I'm really dreaming. They are soft, warm, understanding. I've never been looked at like that before. The feeling makes my heart feel raw, unguarded.

I wind my fingers into her curls and kiss her, even as the part of me watching this happen resists, struggling against the action in the dream, before giving in.

She is the sweetest thing I've ever tasted.

TEN

> Your sparkling eyes / Make me feel better / Reality loses its power"
>
> — "Our Summer," TOMORROW X TOGETHER

BYUNHO

THE NEXT MORNING, Sky knocks on my door to do my makeup. She's wearing a dark green sundress, sandals, and a pair of sunglasses on top of her head, her hair braided back. My heart thuds when I see her, unable to forget the dream that I had last night.

I've never had a dream like that before.

I hold still and try not to meet her eyes as she does my makeup for a second time. I don't mess with her this time. I don't know what I might do if she responded to my teasing. I feel off-balance, unsure. Not like myself.

"We have a long day today. Let's go have some fun!" Yeojin chirps, as usual ignoring Sky's presence. I hope Sky misses the annoyed look that Yeojin gives her when she slides into the cab beside me.

My chest tightens with a strange sensation, burning like anger. I don't like the way that Yeojin is treating Sky.

The cab takes us the short distance to Yongdusan Park, where the Busan Tower is. We stroll around the park and film for about thirty minutes, then do the same for an hour at Gamcheon Culture Village, with its colorful buildings and street art. We climb multiple hills, getting panoramic views of the mountains, buildings, and water beyond.

Everything is going relatively smoothly, until Yeojin snaps at Sky to get out of one of the shots.

Again, that strange sensation in my chest. I recognize it now. I feel protective of Sky.

I could write it off, say that it's the same way I feel protective of the maknaes or my little sister. But it's not the same.

I stop us at the next cafe I see. "What do you want?" I ask Sky, gesturing at the menu. "I'll buy it for you."

"You don't have to do that," she says, blinking at me in surprise. Does she really think I wouldn't do something nice for her?

"Pick something." I hear my voice come out harsher than I intend it to. I soften it. "I want to get something for you."

"We have to keep going, there's lots more to do," Yeojin huffs impatiently when she realizes I have no intention of ordering anything for myself. I shoot her a look of contempt, which gags her—she shuts up for the first time all morning.

Sky smiles gratefully as she sips the disgustingly creamy, too sugary concoction she chose.

The next stop is Jagalchi Market, where we try various street foods for lunch. Sky's mood seems to have lifted, and she asks me questions about the foods she sees, delighted by some and horrified by others, like the beef intestine, which amuses me. I stop and sign an autograph for a teenage girl with her mother. Yeojin is more reserved now and sticks to filming.

After lunch, we take a bus to Taejongdae Resort Park and walk along the cliffside path. The wind off the ocean blows stray strands of my hair that fell out of my ponytail into my face, but serves as a relief from the stifling heat. We linger by the lighthouse and enjoy the view, taking a short break from filming while Yeojin takes a phone call. Sky leans against the railing, lifting her face to the sunlight.

Out of the blue, Sky asks, "So why did you wish to make music and be famous? You said yesterday, at the temple, that's what you wished for."

I think seriously about her question. "Music–all art– makes people's lives better. Including mine. I learned to play guitar and keyboard when I was young and got into rap music and performing... I didn't want to end up like a lot of the other people I knew back then... So I moved to Seoul when I was barely sixteen with only a little money from doing delivery for my Eomma's restaurant. I had no back up plan. I signed on with the first company that would take me as a trainee. That's where I met Changmin."

"That must have been hard. I had no idea your situation was like that." Her eyes are soft with compassion.

I shift the subject from me to her. "And you? What made you move across the world?"

For some reason, she laughs. "Well, my best friend is here. My fashion internship in New York definitely wasn't paying the bills. You know, I did everything I was supposed to when I went to college. I was going to be a lawyer like my parents. But I was so unhappy." She pauses and sighs, tucking a curl behind her ear self-consciously. My eyes follow the movement. "I only started being happy when I stopped doing what other people wanted me to do, and did what I wanted to do instead. No matter how far-fetched it is, someday I want to have my own fashion brand."

My mouth curves. "I think that's a great dream."

Her eyes brighten as she looks over at me. "Really?"

"Yes. Really."

SKY

"I'm so tired of walking," I admit to Byunho with a laugh as we're on our way to our last destination. "I can't remember the last time I walked this much in two days." I don't mean to complain, but Yeojin seems to take it that way.

"No more walking," Yeojin says, a sour look on her face. She's seemed increasingly annoyed all day, and I have no idea why. Maybe because since yesterday, Byunho has been paying more attention to me than to her.

I see what she means when I see the Songdo Cable Car, which are small carriages that run along a cable suspended over the water. We stand in line for so long that I take the opportunity for a bathroom break. But when I come back, Yeojin only has two tickets.

"Both of you will go together," she announces, to my surprise. "You can take photos or video with the camera. I will wait."

Byunho and I look at each other. He shrugs, a slight smirk on his lips that Yeojin doesn't see. We get into one of the cable cars. The space isn't too small for Yeojin to come with us, but I have to admit I'm glad she didn't.

BYUNHO

"What on earth did you say to make her leave us alone?" Sky asks me once we're in the air.

"Nothing," I lie.

Sky crosses her arms over her chest and stares flatly at me.

"While you were in the bathroom, I told her I didn't appreciate her being rude to you, and that it's impacting the quality of the film that we're getting." I smirk.

She gasps. "You didn't have to do that." She even looks like she feels bad for Yeojin.

Those words strike a chord in me. For some reason, I don't want Sky to think badly of me. "You think I'm an asshole for standing up for you?" I ask, despite myself. I look away from her, out the window, like I don't care what she says.

Sky doesn't answer right away. "No, I don't think you are," she finally says, quietly.

I glance back at her. Her wide brown eyes are sincere. She continues, "Actually, I think you care a lot more than you let on."

Not knowing what to say, I say nothing. It feels like she's exposed a part of me that I've kept concealed for a long time.

ELEVEN

> " Pull me dangerously / I'm falling into it / I can't control it"
>
> — "Kiss," NCT Doejaejung

SKY

THE FIFTEEN MINUTE ride one way provides stunning views of the city and shoreline. The water and sky are bright blue, and the mountains around the city are green. I can't stop smiling as we begin the ride back.

"This has been such a beautiful trip," I say as the cable car begins its slow progression back over the water. The sun is setting on our third day in Busan. The colors tonight are especially vibrant, red and orange and deep purple streaking the sky. "You know, I think my supervisor sent me here with you just to get me out of her way. But I'm glad I'm here. This is an amazing city... You're lucky you got to grow up here."

I look back at Byunho, who's watching me thoughtfully.

We're sitting so close now, our legs and arms are touching, and I'm acutely aware of every inch of space between us.

"What?" I manage to ask, though speaking is hard with the way he's looking at me. The same way he did last night at the restaurant, eyes dark and intent. My heart beats faster.

"I just realized that I've enjoyed this city more in two days with you than I did in my entire life."

Those words knock the breath out of me. I stare at him, speechless. The air between us is filled with electricity. Byunho's eyes flicker to my lips, then back to my eyes. I can't breathe. His hand comes up to touch the side of my face, light fingertips along my jaw.

I feel like I'm being pulled by gravity towards him as he tips my face up toward his. My eyes flutter closed as his lips brush ever so lightly against mine.

BYUNHO

The kiss lasts only a moment before Sky pulls away, shaking her head as if to clear it.

"I don't understand!" she exclaims. "I thought you didn't like me. Now you're acting like I'm your friend... then kissing me—"

I can't help but laugh.

She stares at me. "You don't get how that's confusing for me at all?"

"Do you need me to spell it out?" I shake my head in disbelief that she's had no idea this whole time. "Yes, I like you, Sky. And I've wanted to kiss you for days."

Sky searches my face, her brown eyes glowing a dark, melted amber from the day's last beams of sunlight. "Did you just want to kiss me?"

I hold her gaze. The cable car is only a couple minutes away from the ground. "No," I admit. My thoughts about her for the past couple days have been far from pure. "But that's up to you to decide. Do you want more?"

TWELVE

" Knowing but pretending that we don't / We're falling for each other / We already know, losing control"

— "Light a Flame," SEVENTEEN

SKY

I CAN'T BELIEVE what just happened.

Byunho kissed me.

And I kissed him back.

It was the most exhilarating kiss of my life, and also the most terrifying. I don't know what will happen next between us. The way his voice dropped when he admitted he wanted more than to kiss me... my heart hasn't stopped racing.

When we got off the cable car only a couple minutes later, it seems so obvious what we've been doing, my face flushed with heat. Thankfully, Byunho is a better actor than I am. He shows no outward sign that anything happened, seeming just as unbothered as ever.

We find Yeojin standing near the exit with her arms crossed, waiting for us. "That's all for filming. I'll put all the footage together, you don't need to do anything else. I've called a taxi to take you wherever you need to go."

"It was good working with you," Byunho says politely. He sneaks a glance at me out of the corner of his eye, and I try not to laugh, high on the feeling of how he looks at me.

* * *

BYUNHO ASKS the taxi driver to take us somewhere other than our hotel. We get out and Byunho asks the taxi driver to wait, paying him more. "Where are you taking me?" I ask with false suspicion, and his show he's smirking beneath his mask as takes my hand. The touch sends sparks racing up my arm, spreading warmth through the rest of my body. I don't pull away.

"I hope you don't mind a little more walking," he says. "There's somewhere we haven't been yet that I think you might like."

I groan with a laugh. "I'm so tired, but I can deal with another short walk."

We find ourselves at a place called Igidae Park, and I don't understand why Byunho brought me here until we reach the top of a set of lit wooden stairs leading down to a waterfront. The ocean is dark blue and crashing on the rocks below, with the glittering buildings of the city and mountains set behind it, beneath the dusky blue sky. All of my fatigue from the day eases with the fresh sea breeze, and we walk for a little while side by side, only stopping to lean against the railing and look out at the water.

Byunho lounges with his elbows on the railing, relaxed and himself, no longer putting on a show for the camera.

"You were right, this place is nice." I shiver, not prepared for the chilly night breeze.

He notices and takes off his jacket, placing it around my shoulders. "Thank you," I say. He leans his bare arms on the railing beside me again. He must be cold, but I know better than to make him take his jacket back. As another moment passes, I can't ignore the elephant in the room any longer.

"We leave for Seoul in the morning," I say, then stop. I don't know what else to say about the situation. Obviously, I can't expect him to drop everything and be my boyfriend. I'm not naive. Even though he no longer has a dating ban, we still work together. And maybe this isn't that serious to him. I'm getting way ahead of myself. It doesn't need to be serious.

After I trail off into silence, he says, "You still haven't answered my question."

Oh. *Do you want more?* His eyes are dark and focused on me. I can't hold his gaze, and I can't answer the question directly. My heart races, sending a current of heat throughout my body.

"I want you to kiss me again," something possesses me to say.

His eyes darken. I can't breathe as he leans in, brushing his lips against mine like before.

It's like a dam breaks, and my desire comes flooding through me like a tidal wave. I gasp against his lips, and Byunho makes a sound in the back of his throat. One hand wraps around the back of my neck and his other hand holds my waist. He pulls me closer, deepening the kiss as his mouth devours mine. I can feel his heart pounding just as hard as mine underneath my hand.

Breathless, we finally break apart. I can't seem to find anything to say to him, my head spinning. He smiles slightly. "Are you hungry?"

A few drops of water start to fall from the sky. We'd been

lucky with weather so far on our trip, but it's now starting to rain. We run the rest of the way back to the waiting taxi.

The last destination is a tiny hole-in-the-wall restaurant which turns out to have some of the best food I've tasted on this trip, better even than the fancy restaurant we ate at last night. I inhale the seafood noodle soup we ordered. When we're done, Byunho and I split a bottle of soju. It's not my favorite since I'm not a big drinker, but I think it could grow on me.

"Should we go back to the hotel?" Byunho asks when we're done eating.

I nod in response.

That's all it takes – he pays the check, and we take a taxi back to the hotel. In the cab, he doesn't even look at me as he runs his fingertips over the backs of my knuckles, hand, and wrist. I think I might go insane from that small touch, but I don't want it to stop.

Back at the hotel, we step inside the empty elevator and he selects our floor number calmly. The doors close. Overcome with a sudden boldness, I close the space between us. He only has a moment to be surprised before I reach up, wrapping my arms around his shoulders and pulling his face down to mine.

BYUNHO

In the elevator, Sky presses her body against mine and kisses me. Her hands sink into the longer hair at the back of my neck. Her forwardness adds fuel to the fire blazing inside me, turning it to a roaring inferno.

I pull her closer, her mouth opening against mine. Sliding my tongue against hers, she makes a small, needy sound that makes any semblance of my self-control turn to ashes. "You're playing with fire," I murmur warningly, drawing away slightly to fix her with a matching look.

The elevator dings.

We spring apart as the doors open and a man in a suit gets into the elevator. I try to calm my breathing, cursing the man out in my mind and glaring daggers at the back of his head.

Sky smooths her dress, but I can see her hands trembling. I don't hide my smirk of satisfaction.

At our floor, we exit the elevator. Down the hall in one direction is my room, and down the hall the other direction is her room. Sky glances at me, a question in her eyes.

SKY

The corner of Byunho's mouth turns up. "Come with me," he murmurs.

My heart pounds as I follow him, the space between us charged. My stomach flips over as we reach the door to his room and he unlocks it with his key card. I step inside.

Before the door has clicked fully shut, Byunho grabs me and kisses me, hard, the force of it causing my back to bump into the wall. One of his hands comes up to rest on the side of my neck, just beneath my jaw, while the other grabs onto my hip. His teeth tease my bottom lip. I gasp and wrap my arms around his back, pulling him even closer, trying to close the space between our bodies as his tongue tangles with mine.

His hand on my hip slides lower, sliding beneath the hem of my dress and then gripping the side of my thigh. I shudder and slide my hands under the back of his shirt. The muscles beneath the smooth skin of his back flex against my palms as he draws back to look at me in the darkness of the room, his hand releasing my thigh. "You want this?" he asks me, voice husky.

My lips feel swollen from kissing. "Where do I sign?" I manage to joke. I feel drunk, but the small amount of soju we drank wasn't nearly enough to make me intoxicated. It's him, his touch, that's intoxicating.

My pulse pounds with an overwhelming mixture of desire and nervousness, and a small amount of clarity pushes through the fog of my desire.

He's two years older than me, and though I'm not inexperienced exactly, joking about signing an NDA makes me realize he's still probably more experienced than I am. He's probably been with many beautiful women. Who was that female idol he had a dating rumor with again? I don't want to be insecure, but I can't help but think about it.

Byunho chuckles at my half-delirious attempt at humor. "Don't worry about that." He flicks on the light switch beside my head, which turns on the lamps on either side of the king-sized bed, so we're no longer standing in the shadows. I can finally see his face, and he can see mine. He's so beautiful, it hurts to look at him this close. He leans over me with his arms caging me in on either side of my head.

His dark eyes study me. The intensity with which he's looking at me is enough to make me forget my feelings of insecurity from a moment before. I can feel my pulse throbbing and wetness between my thighs.

Byunho's lips curve into a smirk. "I'm still waiting for a yes." He arches a dark brow.

Jerk. I release a ragged breath and close the distance between us. "Yes," I whisper against his lips.

THIRTEEN

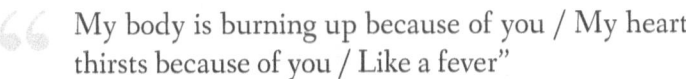 My body is burning up because of you / My heart thirsts because of you / Like a fever"

— "Fever," ENHYPEN

SKY

BYUNHO GROWLS and hauls me against him, picking me up with shocking ease. Our teeth clack together with the roughness of the kiss as his tongue strokes against mine. I wrap my arms around his neck and my legs around his waist as he carries me to the bed and lowers me down onto the edge of it.

I try to catch my breath as he steps back, his hands tracing down my calves. I lift my head to watch him remove my sandals and kick off his sneakers. I scoot back further on the bed to make room for him. He climbs onto the bed, kneeling between my legs. His hands skim up my sides, riding my dress up to my waist.

I slip my own hands up beneath his shirt, tugging on the hem. He helps by pulling his shirt off over his head. I slide my hands up his stomach and chest while he stays still, letting me explore the firm planes of his lean muscles with my hands. With my fingertips, I trace the star-shaped tattoo on his hip, KOSMIC's logo.

"Your turn," Byunho says, and I obligingly use his bare shoulders as leverage to sit up so he can pull my dress off over my head. He tosses it aside and his eyes devour my body, covered only by a black bra and matching panties. He lifts a hand, grasping one of my breasts through my bra before sliding his hand up to the juncture of my collarbone and neck, his thumb resting gently at the base of my throat as he tips my head back and kisses me.

His other hand expertly undoes the clasp of my bra while he kisses me. He slides the straps off my shoulders and tosses my bra aside, then cups my breasts in his hands, thumbs circling the peaked nipples. I shiver and reach for the button on his pants, but he grabs my wrist, stopping me with a raised brow. "Not yet. Lie down."

I do what he says, my heart pounding wildly. His fingers tuck into the elastic waistband of my panties, and he tugs them down over my ass and thighs, down my legs, and off.

My breathing catches as he turns the intensity of his gaze to the most private part of me. He loops his arms beneath my knees, shifting my hips toward him, and lowers his face to the juncture between my legs. He kisses me there teasingly, and I try not to whimper. He tastes me slowly, taking his time. "You taste good," he murmurs, just before his tongue finds my clit, making my body jerk involuntarily.

His tongue is deft as he teases the sensitive bud, finding the motions that draw helpless sounds of pleasure from me. The last coherent thought I have is that being a rapper makes you good with your tongue.

I bunch my hands in his dark red hair, weaving my fingers

through the longer strands that brush my hips. My mind floats away from my body, lost in building sensation. I come apart.

BYUNHO

When Sky is limp with pleasure, I lift my head and sit up, savoring the taste of her on my lips and the sight of her spread before me. Her smooth limbs are sprawled across the bed, her legs fallen open without any measure of self-consciousness left. Just how I want her.

She raises her head to look at me, a dark curl falling across her cheek. "Please," she whimpers. "I need you."

My lips curve with satisfaction.

SKY

Climbing off the bed, Byunho unbuttons his pants and strips off the rest of his clothing. He turns to search for something in his suitcase, giving me a perfect view of his butt, muscularly toned from dancing. I rise up onto my elbows to get a better look.

He finds what he was looking for—a condom in a small foil package.

He then kneels between my legs once more. My whole body throbs with the need to have him inside of me. I watch as he tears open the package and rolls the condom over his cock.

Everything Byunho does is slow and deliberate, watching my reactions with an intensity that makes me breathless. He grasps my thigh with one hand, my hip with the other, and slowly sinks into the center of me. The smooth, hard length of him feels incredible. But he moves slowly, easing into me, being too gentle. I arch against him and grab onto his hips with my hands, pulling him deeper into me.

He groans and squeezes his eyes shut with concentration. "Sky. You're making it hard for me to go slow."

"Don't hold back," I beg, moving my hips against his. "I can take it."

He opens his eyes. An evil smirk twists his lips. He lifts my hips as he thrusts harder into me, making me gasp. "Like that?"

I make an incoherent noise of agreement, and Byunho stops holding back, fucking me with a steady, relentless rhythm that hits just the right spot inside of me.

Even though he's holding on to me, I've ended up pushed back against the mound of pillows at the head of the bed. Lost in sensation, all I can do is admire how beautiful he is. The way his muscles flex beneath his sun-kissed skin, the sweat forming on his brow, the way he throws his head back, eyes closing, as he moans my name and curses in the same breath. "Sky. Fuck."

His pace quickens, and I cry out involuntarily as the wave of sensation slams into me suddenly, washing over me with incredible intensity. I hang suspended in that feeling for a long moment while he pounds into me. He groans as he joins me, riding the wave as it comes crashing down together.

BYUNHO

Sky's eyes flutter open to watch me climb off the bed. "Be right back," I say. My legs are a bit unsteady as I walk to the bathroom.

I clean myself up and when I come back out, Sky is sitting up, hugging a pillow to her chest, chewing her bottom lip in uncertainty. So I cross the room to her, and leaning over the bed, tip her chin up with my fingers, kissing her gently on the mouth.

"You can stay here tonight," I clarify. I go to my suitcase and find a clean, oversized t-shirt for her to wear, which I toss at her.

She catches it against her chest, smiling shyly, and pulls it on over her head. I get another glimpse of her beautiful body as she does.

I put on a clean pair of boxers and climb into the bed beside her, hiding my own discomfort with this intimacy by pretending it's not a big deal to me. Saying nothing, I turn off the lights and lay back against the pillows in the dark, acutely aware of her presence beside me.

She shifts closer, pressing her body against mine. I don't move. As her breathing deepens and she falls asleep, she nestles closer, tucking her head against my shoulder and throwing her arm across my stomach.

I don't pull away.

FOURTEEN

<blockquote>
"Baby, we're a scandal / Way too hot to handle"

— "Scandal," TWICE
</blockquote>

SKY

I WAKE ENVELOPED in pleasant warmth, the sound of an unfamiliar alarm blaring somewhere next to me. My pillow shifts slightly, and the sound stops, allowing me to relax again.

It takes me another moment of drowsy bliss to realize that the source of the delicious warmth is a man whose pecs I'm currently using as a pillow.

The events of the previous night flood my mind, and suddenly I'm wide awake, heart pounding. I lift my head and find myself face to face with Byunho, whose red hair is mussed and his eyes still half-closed. "Mm," he murmurs, his rough morning voice making a deep rumble that reverberates through his chest.

"Hi," I say shyly, pressing my lips together in embarrassment. I roll over so I'm facing away from him.

He sighs deeply, before the bed shifts and I feel his warmth disappear as he gets up. "We have to go back to Seoul today."

Right. No time to be obsessing over what happened last night, although I have no idea how I'm going to pretend it didn't happen. I push myself into a sitting position, the sheet falling down to my waist, and realize that my suitcase is in my room, and I have nothing to wear but the clothes I wore last night, on the floor.

Byunho comes out of the bathroom wearing a pair of knee-length shorts and a t-shirt. He clears his throat. "I can get your things for you," he says. There's an awkwardness between us now that wasn't there last night.

"My key card is in my bag," I say, pointing to where it sits on the desk. "Thanks."

As I wait for him to come back, I climb out of bed, padding into the bathroom to splash water on my face and attempt to clear my thoughts.

Never could I have predicted that something like this would happen with Byunho. Not that long ago, I thought he couldn't stand me. But nothing about what happened last night feels like he hates me.

Things are different. And I have no idea what happens next.

BYUNHO

We check out of our rooms and leave Busan behind. A part of me aches with the pain of leaving my mother and sister behind. But that feeling is familiar. This other feeling that I now have is not.

Sky sits in the passenger seat, staring at her phone or out the window and trying hard, I think, not to make eye contact with me. Maybe she regrets what happened last night. Maybe she wants nothing more to do with me. My chest pangs at the thought, making me grip the steering wheel with white knuckles.

I don't know how to discuss any of this with her.

"How are you feeling?" I finally ask, keeping my voice neutral and casual.

I feel Sky's gaze on my face as I focus on the road. "Oh, I'm feeling fine." She laughs, the sound sweet. "How about you?"

"Better than fine." My mouth twitches into a smirk, and I glance over just in time to see her cheeks flush.

"So, um," she says after a moment of silence. Then she asks a question that I've been dreading. "What happens when we get back to Seoul?"

SKY

Byunho's eyes are steady on the road. "No one can know what happened between us," he finally says, then cuts a glance at me. "Not even Kim Aera. Not even my members."

My initial reaction is a pain in my chest. On the one hand, I understand that it's not personal and he wants to keep our relationship — whatever it is — outwardly professional because he's a celebrity. But it feels personal to me, because maybe I care too much. I let my emotions into something that, to him, might have just been physical. How am I not supposed to show how much I like him? How am I not supposed to tell Aera about us? But even though I haven't signed an NDA or anything, I wouldn't betray his trust by telling anyone.

"Okay," I agree. "I won't tell anyone, I promise."

* * *

AFTER THAT, my efforts at conversation go nowhere. It's like Byunho has put up a wall with no doors or windows. Despite my best efforts to stay awake, I fall asleep a couple hours into the ride.

I wake to Byunho's voice and the light touch of his hand on my arm, which he pulls away as soon as I lift my head. "We're outside your apartment," he says, expression unreadable.

"Oh." I rub my eyes and grab my purse from the floor before clambering out of his fancy car. He gets out too.

"Do you need help carrying anything?"

"Oh, no, I've got it." We stand awkwardly next to the Lambo. I feel like I might go insane if I have to look at him for another moment. "Well, see you later then!" I say, and make myself walk away like everything that happened between us means nothing to me.

After shutting the door to my cramped studio apartment behind me, I let out a long sigh and wonder what the hell I'm going to do. The first step is turning my fan on, because of how stuffy the place got while I was away. I collapse onto my beanbag.

My mind swirls with thoughts, the secret of what happened in Busan burning inside of me. And yet I have to go back to work tomorrow morning like nothing happened.

I text Aera that I'm back home, then take a shower and fix myself something to eat. By then, Aera has texted me back, suggesting we meet for lunch the next day.

It will be good to see her, even if I can't tell her anything.

BYUNHO

Instead of going back to the dorms, after I drop Sky off, I go straight to my studio at the CKM building. It's a private room with sound-proofed walls and a lock on the door.

When KOSMIC first debuted, we had to schedule private studio time to work on producing with access to all of the best equipment. Now, I have a studio that's all mine, with equipment that I own. It's the place that I go to be alone, think, or in my current state, try to distract myself from how I'm feeling.

I pour all of my emotions into my music until hours have passed.

* * *

"YOU'RE BACK JUST IN TIME," Tai says when I get to the dorm late that night. It's almost 1 a.m., but he and Changmin are in the living room. When I came in, their heads were bent together over a notebook while trying not to let the sheet masks they're wearing slide off. The sight would be amusing if I weren't so distracted. Come to think of it, they've been spending a lot of time together. Although maybe that's nothing new.

"How was Busan?" Changmin asks.

"Fine," I say shortly. The two of them glance at each other, their real expressions hidden beneath their ridiculous-looking sheet masks. I ignore this reaction, not having the energy to care about what they think, and go to my room.

While I'm brushing my teeth, Haru opens the door to the bathroom, raising his brows in surprise to see me there. He's wearing his pajamas already, his dark bangs falling into his eyes.

"Have you heard of privacy?" I grumble, make room for him at the sink.

Haru shrugs innocently and grabs his own toothbrush.

None of us really care about our privacy with one another at this point. We've all seen each other naked, sick, or any other state. Haru is just like the bothersome little brother I never had. Jaesung is like his evil twin.

"Hyung, did you apologize to Miss Sky?" he asks.

I try not to choke on my toothpaste at the mention of Sky's name. "I did. On the last day of filming the music video."

Haru speaks around his toothbrush. "So did the trip with her go well?"

My brow creases. "How did you find out about that?" I lean over the sink to spit out the toothpaste.

"Tai hyung."

That's how hard it is to keep secrets in a group like this. Which is exactly why I can't let any of my members know that anything is going on with me and Sky.

I don't answer his question, but the thought of her stays in my mind for the rest of the night, like her whispered voice. The memory of kissing her is like a permanent tattoo on my lips.

PART 2

"Because you are my stars and my universe
These hardships are just temporary
Just shine as bright as you shine now"

— "My Universe," Coldplay ft. BTS

FIFTEEN

> " Feeling far away, come a little closer, hey / But if
> you're unsure / I'm not gonna be the one to get
> hurt"
>
> — "Hurt," New Jeans

SKY

THE RESTAURANT where I meet Aera for lunch the next
day is one of our regular lunch destinations because it's walking
distance from the office and its sandwiches are delicious. I snag
a seat by a window. Then I wait for her to arrive, her bodyguard
following a short distance behind her and sitting down a couple
tables away as usual.

She sinks down into the chair opposite me and lets out a
long sigh that sounds like relief. She's wearing a white button-
down dress and pointed beige heels, dark tinted sunglasses and
a mask. "How was going to Busan?" she asks, pushing her
sunglasses on top of her head and reaching for the iced coffee I
ordered for her.

I pause too long before I speak, because I don't know how to act like a normal person when I'm trying to lie to my best friend. "Oh, it was really fun actually. I got to explore all over the city. We went to a temple, the beach, saw a part of the city with pretty murals, and rode on a cable car... And Byunho was a perfect, um, gentleman."

I'm not lying, but I am keeping a huge secret from her. And that's kind of lying. My palms start to sweat.

"That's good. You'll be paid extra for your time, I made sure of it. These sorts of things do happen, but Manager Sangjin really should have picked an assistant manager to go, or Stylist Goh could have picked a makeup artist to send instead." Aera sighs.

At that moment the waiter circles back to our table and we place our lunch orders. "I'll also be paying for whatever that man orders," Aera adds, gesturing to the table where her bodyguard sits. The waiter nods and leaves.

"What about you?" I ask.

Aera smiles shyly, knowing that I mean her and Hajun. She looks down, tapping her neatly manicured nails on the table as if she's nervous about what she's going to say. "Actually, I asked him to move in together."

My mouth drops open. "That's a big deal." Aera currently still lives with her father in the house she grew up in, which I know is difficult for her.

I've been over there a few times since moving here. The first time, I was shocked by the scale of the place, the garage full of luxury cars and the sleek modern interior of the house mostly lacking in personal touches like family photographs or souvenirs from vacations. It's not a very warm or welcoming place, other than her bedroom which is apparently about the same as it was when she was in high school.

"Are you going to talk to your dad about it?"

"No. That wouldn't go well." Aera shakes her head.

Before her mood can fall, I suggest that she come have dinner at my apartment at some point soon. Aera brightens at my idea and the rest of our lunch is spent discussing lighter topics.

"Bye, have a good week! Can't wait to hang out soon." I wave goodbye to her outside the company building.

Our lunch date almost took my mind off of Byunho. Almost.

* * *

KOSMIC'S COMEBACK is happening in only two weeks, which means that we have that much time to wrap up putting together outfits for a month of comeback performance stages and variety show appearances. In that time, the music video is getting edited and the physical albums are being manufactured to hit the shelves right when it drops. The guys are practicing the choreography for the new songs and pre-filming content that will be released during the promotions.

The days after coming back from Busan are all spent in what I've affectionately nicknamed the "fashion cave," the huge warehouse-like room of the CKM building where we do most of our work as stylists.

Stylist Goh works with the fashion PR representative to select which brand items will be going into outfits, and the other assistant stylists and I all try to fit the pieces together into multiple individual outfits that fit the concept for each stage. I can make alterations and create custom pieces, too, with Ms. Goh's permission.

Ms. Goh then decides whether the outfits form a cohesive image as a group and picks the best ones, ensuring that the fashion of every performance is unique and striking.

Every morning I take the subway for forty or fifty minutes to work, crossing the Han River from Itaewon to Gangnam. I spend my day picking out Byunho's outfits by imagining him in each one. I imagine how the jacket would hug his shoulders, how the pants would ride on his hips. Features that I know more intimately than I should.

I try not to think about him too much, although not thinking about him is impossible. After each day, I ride the subway back to my tiny apartment, wishing my commute were just a bit shorter.

I don't know what's worse, not seeing Byunho or seeing him. I'm not sure if he has my number, but would he even text me or call me if he did?

BYUNHO

"You have to come out further as you do this move," Tai says to Simon, stopping our run-through of the set briefly to correct the younger member's position on the stage. "Otherwise you won't be close enough for me to pass you the mic."

It's happening. Our first comeback as a group since Hajun left. Starting with a comeback showcase concert tonight for members of our fanclub, Infinity, the album will be released tomorrow night, followed by a month of promotions.

We've already practiced the choreography to our new and old songs a million times. This rehearsal is focused on tuning up our formations for this stage.

"Okay, I've got it." Simon pushes his bangs impatiently away from his glasses.

"Let's run through it again," Tai says. In our group, he is in charge of dance performance. Along with Haru (and Hajun, before), he works with choreographers to design a lot of our dances. As for me, I'm not bad by any means, but I'm not on the same level as those three.

The bright stage light shines on us before the empty concert hall as we run through the new song one more time. Staff members adjust equipment in the background.

"Don't get complacent just because the album pre-sales are good," we were told yesterday in a meeting with management. "Your group is in a hard position. You lost your most popular member. Fans might be unsure about the band now. Give it your all and convince them you're even better than before."

What they weren't saying was that we need to convince the company, too. Our chance of getting another world tour depends on the company's assessment of this comeback's success.

After wrapping up our rehearsal, we head down the stairs at the side of the stage. The Infinities will be let into the venue in about two and a half hours, just long enough for us to get changed into our stage outfits and get hair and makeup done.

The backstage of the smallish concert venue owned by CKM Entertainment is a maze of hallways and a large room with scaffolding beneath and behind the stage where crew bustle about preparing for the mini-concert.

I trail behind my members as we head toward the dressing area, my pulse picking up at the thought of seeing Sky for the first time since I said goodbye to her outside her apartment. Ahead of me, Simon ruffles Jaesung's blond hair in a moment of affection while Changmin and Haru discuss the performance ahead. Tai falls back to walk beside me silently.

Tai must think that I'm nervous about the performance, or maybe he's nervous as well. What makes him a good roommate and coworker is that we can both exist in silence together. And that makes him a good friend, too.

We walk into the dressing room. My eyes immediately go to Sky as if she were the center of a spotlight on a dark stage.

Her back is facing me as she speaks with another stylist, both of them organizing a rack of clothes holding our stage outfits. I can see her face in one of the vanity mirrors along the wall. Her eyes catch mine in the mirror, and it feels like a rush of adrenaline in my veins.

SKY

Byunho was staring at me a moment ago. Now he's looking anywhere but at me as he's handed his first stage outfit by Stylist Eunjung.

My stomach sinks as I accept this might be what it's going to be like between us from now on. Never admitting what happened between us, even to each other.

I debate whether or not to give him the thing I made for him, and when to give it to him.

The other members say hi to me before they go to change. I spend the next hour making a couple small adjustments on Jaesung's and Tai's outfits.

Jaesung asks me a million questions about Busan, mostly about the food, while I try to ignore the fact that Byunho is only a few paces away in a chair getting his hair and makeup done. Nearby, Simon and Haru do vocal exercises together to warm up, and yet, Byunho sitting silently is somehow more distracting.

Tai barely says anything as I stand in front of him trying to figure out how to make sure his jacket doesn't pop open while he's dancing, which could be a problem just because he's so muscular and this fabric doesn't stretch well. "It's okay if it happens," Tai tells me with a shrug. "Infinities like it."

I smile back. "It's nice that you think about what they like," I say. "But my job is making sure your clothes *don't* fall off, hopefully... Okay, you should be good." I step back to survey my work.

A commotion sounds as Jaesung jumps up from his nearby seat with a yell of happiness.

Standing in the doorway is KOSMIC's former member and Aera's boyfriend, Hajun.

SIXTEEN

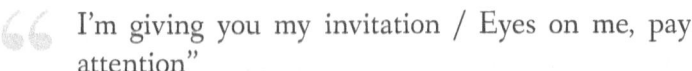 I'm giving you my invitation / Eyes on me, pay attention"

— "Fireworks (I'm the One)," ATEEZ

BYUNHO

HAJUN WALKS into the dressing room, smiling, and the members get up to greet him.

"What are you doing here?" Changmin asks, grinning as he hugs our former group mate.

"I just stopped by to watch your showcase and wish you luck," Hajun says.

My hair stylist puts a hand on my shoulder to prevent me from getting up, although I'm not in any hurry. "One more minute, almost done," she says.

Sky glances over at me, and our eyes meet once again in the mirror. Caught, she jerks her gaze away from mine and busies herself with a task on the other side of the room, as far away from me as she can get.

We need to talk again, but now isn't the time.

When my hair is finally done, I walk over to Hajun and the other members. The last time I saw him in person was about a month ago. He's still in our casual, non-work group chat, although Hajun and I interact more by sending song demos back and forth than texting, since I don't use the group chat as often as everyone else. It feels strange for him to be here when he's not going to be performing with us.

He's a living reminder that it's dangerous to let my feelings get involved with Sky.

"Hey, hyung," Hajun says. I clasp his arm in greeting. "Nice hair," he adds, smirking at my long red hair, half of it up in a ponytail and the other half down. He knows how much I hate dyeing my hair.

I snort. "My scalp has seen better days. Can't wait to chop it all off and start over." I've been growing it out for a year.

"Ten minutes, you should all get to the stage," Manager Sangjin says, striding into the room and tapping his wrist watch. He does a double take when he sees Hajun and gives him a nod, which Hajun returns.

Buzzing with anticipation, everyone starts moving out of the room.

"Wait," says a familiar voice that makes my pulse skip. I stop to find Sky standing beside me. "This necklace is supposed to go with your outfit." She holds up a chunky silver chain with a row of shiny metal beads alternating with glass beads. A tiny star pendant dangles from a smaller chain in the front. She bites her lip as she looks at me, as if she's worried I'm going to refuse.

With a nod, I turn so that she can put it on. Her fingers brush the back of my neck as she reaches up and moves my hair aside, and a shiver of desire courses through me. How can just a simple touch from her make me feel lose my senses so completely?

After a couple of seconds she fastens the clasp, the weight of it settling around my neck, and I turn around. "Did you make this?" I ask, touching the tiny star that brushes against my collarbone, just over my heart.

"Yes, I finished it last night," she says, looking up at me with that same hesitant expression in her beautiful brown eyes. We stand so close now that it would be nothing to lean down and kiss her. It takes every scrap of sense I have left to restrain myself.

"Then I hope you're okay with not getting it back," I say, dropping my hand from the necklace. I step back from her and jog toward the stage.

The members wait by the side of the stage, waiting to go on. Hajun stands with them. "Good, you're here," Changmin says. We circle up for our pre-show ritual, naturally leaving room for Hajun. After a second of hesitation, Changmin asks, "Hajun, do you want to do the honors?"

Hajun's throat moves as he swallows, but he steps into the gap in our circle and puts his hand in next to ours. "1, 2, 3," he counts out, and we all chant in unison, "KOSMIC!"

SKY

I stand there for a moment after Byunho leaves, at a loss for predicting that man's behavior. Despite myself, I can't help but feel giddy that he wants to keep the necklace that I made for him. Even if it means nothing to him and everything to me.

With nothing to do except be on standby, I grab a box full of things I might need to make emergency repairs, and some hand towels for sweat. I was told to keep these on hand at the side of the stage. Then I head out toward the stage area, excited to watch the performance. That's when Hajun, standing in the offstage area adjacent to the stage, sees me and waves me over with one hand.

I approach, suddenly shy. This is my best friend's boyfriend, but she's not here. I don't know how to act.

"Hey, Sky," Hajun says, smiling slightly. "Come watch with me."

I join him just as the intro music to KOSMIC's new title track "ASTEROID" starts and the members immediately launch into the energetic choreography. Fire shoots out of the front of the stage and the stage lights flash. Tai starts the song out with his rap verse, followed by several lines sung by Jaesung. The screen behind them shows animated space scenes of asteroids, which combined with the fire and lights create the effect of KOSMIC dancing in space. Simon and Haru trade off in the pre-chorus, and Changmin leads the chorus.

As soon as the chorus ends, Byunho's rap verse starts. His energy and charisma as he delivers the verse is captivating, and the smirk he gives the audience makes them scream. I feel my heart pounding as I watch him.

"They're so good," I breathe, and Hajun chuckles, snapping me out of my trance.

"Yeah, they are." There's a note of sadness, or maybe nostalgia, in his voice that makes my heart twinge with sympathy. Smiling slightly, Hajun adds, "But I have no regrets."

I return his smile, both of us sharing the secret of his relationship with Aera. We continue watching performance together, and in those moments I feel a sort of companionship with him that is a little surprising to me.

I can't help but wonder, though, if Byunho has regrets about what's happened between us. I'm not sure how I feel.

* * *

DURING A PAUSE IN THE SHOW, Byunho makes his way off stage toward us, gulping down a bottle of water as he walks. He raises a brow when he sees me standing with Hajun, but then nods toward the box of towels I have.

"Can I get some of those?" he asks, holding my gaze, his voice rough from overuse.

My stomach does a flip as I pass him enough towels for him and the members.

"Thanks," he says, beginning to mop the sweat off his neck. I can't help but look away awkwardly. I think I catch a slight smirk on his mouth as he turns away and strides back on stage, where the other members are chatting with the audience.

Hajun watches the interaction, eyes following Byunho as he leaves, but makes no comment about the tension between me and Byunho. I can only hope he didn't notice anything out of the ordinary.

BYUNHO

"Nice job, everyone," Changmin says, praising the members as we make our way backstage. The show went even better than we'd hoped, including the debut screening of the music video at the end. The fans were happy to see us, and we were grateful to see them. After so long, it was a relief to feel that Infinities still supported us and our music. I think each of us lives with a hidden fear that our fans will disappear if we don't constantly give them new music and content. It's been a long time.

We head back to the dressing area to change out of our stage outfits, shower off, and change back into everyday clothes. I tuck the necklace Sky made me into my t-shirt.

"Hyung! You coming to the after party?" Jaesung asks me as I come out of the changing stall. He means the party they're throwing with a bunch of their idol friends.

"No, thanks," I say. I've gone to plenty of those. I have other plans tonight. My body still thrums from the high of performing on stage. I feel reckless.

SKY

It takes about an hour for me and the rest of the styling team to pack up the stage outfits and other styling equipment. By then it's night, and I still have to take the train home.

As I exit the back door of the venue, a tall figure steps out of the darkness at the bottom of the stairs. I shriek and stumble, nearly falling on my face, but am caught by a pair of strong arms that hold me upright.

"It's me," a familiar deep voice breathes into my ear.

Byunho.

I sag against him in relief, and a moment later he releases me. "What the hell?" I step back and glare at him, heart pounding. "You almost gave me a heart attack."

"Sorry," he says, and it might not be a word he says very often, but he seems to mean it. "I didn't want anyone to see us together, but I wanted to offer to drive you home. I think we should talk."

"Oh." Heat flushes my face. He must have waited here this whole time after the show for me to come out. "You didn't have to do that."

Byunho holds my gaze. "I want to."

"Okay," I agree. "Let's leave before someone sees us."

He leads me the short distance to the private lot where his Lambo is parked, walking beside me. The late summer night breeze is cool enough to give me goosebumps, a sign that it will be autumn soon. When we reach his car, he walks over to the passenger side and opens the door for me. I get in quickly, hoping that no one has seen us.

Byunho gets into the car, and my heart skips a beat as I realize we're alone again for the first time since we got back from the trip to Busan.

SEVENTEEN

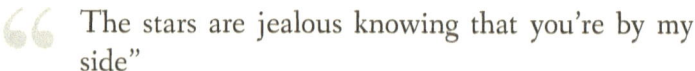 The stars are jealous knowing that you're by my side"

— "Drive (Bangchan, Lee Know)," Stray Kids

SKY

THE ENGINE RUMBLES TO LIFE, and Byunho puts his hand on my headrest to reverse, then pulls out of the parking lot. I let myself look at him, the way his dark red hair is tied back in a ponytail and how his jeans hug his thighs.

My eyes catch on the chain of the necklace I gave him, tucked into his shirt. "You kept the necklace."

"I told you, it's mine." The edge of Byunho's mouth curves up in a grin, cutting his eyes over at me.

I glance away, pretending I wasn't staring at him. "Okay. Since it's not an item on loan from a brand, I guess you can keep it," I say nonchalantly. Technically, it's CKM property, because I used supplies at the office to make it. But I doubt anyone will notice a few missing beads.

"Thank you."

I watch out the window as the buildings of Seoul pass by. The drive from the concert venue to my house is not a short one. Getting into his car again might have been a mistake.

BYUNHO

Now that Sky is in my car, I don't know how to tell her what I want to say. Stalling, I ask, "What did you think of the performance?"

She smiles, the expression lighting up her face in a way that makes my chest fill with a warm satisfaction. "I loved it! All of the new songs are great. I've actually never seen you guys perform live before today."

I glance at her in surprise. "You never went to my concert?"

"Well, no…" Sky mutters, and I realize I've embarrassed her.

"It made me feel good to know you were watching," I admit, the words spilling out of me before I can give any thought to their impact.

Sky falls silent, and I clench my hands around the steering wheel, not daring to look over and see her reaction.

"You were really good," she finally says.

"Am I still your favorite rapper?" I ask, smirking slightly because I can't resist teasing her. It was one of the first things she said to me, when we met at the hotel in New York.

"Oh my god, you still remember that!" Sky covers her face with her hands.

"Of course I do." I glance at her, still smirking. "So, am I?"

She sighs, then shrugs and says unenthusiastically, "Eh, I guess so."

I frown. What sort of answer is that?

A giggle bursts out of her at my expression. My scowl deepens, and she laughs harder.

"That's not funny." I shoot a glare at her, but her laughter is infectious and I can't help but grin as she smiles back.

Impulsively, I take a chance and reach across the console for her hand.

SKY

My stomach flips as, grinning, Byunho takes my left hand in his right, before directing his attention back to the road as if holding my hand is the most natural thing ever.

His hand is warm and strong, fingers wrapped around mine, cradling my hand lightly in his. A metal ring he wears is cool against my skin.

I'm more confused than ever. And yet his touch feels so good that it takes me a long moment and every shred of willpower I have left to pull my hand from his. "I can't do this," I say.

BYUNHO

Sky's words are like a punch to the stomach. *I can't do this.*

"What do you mean?" I ask, looking over at her in alarm. She looks like she's about to cry, and I feel like I can't breathe.

I find a place to pull over, throwing my emergency blinkers on as I turn to her.

"You keep toying with me, and I can't stand it!" she gasps, staring at me with accusation. "You're hot and then you're cold. We sleep together, then you tell me no one can know, and I don't hear from you for weeks." A ragged breath makes her voice catch. "Now you're wearing my necklace and driving me home and trying to hold my hand? I have no idea what you want from me." She shakes her head, an angry tear slipping from the corner of her eye and sliding down her cheek. "Do you have any idea how that feels? It might be a fun game for you to play with my heart, but I won't let you break it. I'll just... take a taxi home."

Sky fumbles with the door and gets out before I can stop her.

"Sky!" I throw open my door and in a few seconds I've caught up to her on the sidewalk. I grab her wrist. She spins around and glares up at me, brown eyes luminous.

SKY

I stumble down the sidewalk, fumbling with my phone to try to call a taxi while tears cloud my vision. The street is mostly empty, only a few cars on the road, no one else walking on the sidewalk this late at night beneath the golden glow of the streetlights.

Byunho catches up to me fast, catching my wrist. Spinning around, I glare at him.

"What are you doing? Someone could see you!"

"I don't care." Byunho takes my face in his hands and kisses me.

My mouth parts in surprise, letting him in. I melt into his touch, his palms spanning either side of my face. Byunho pulls away just enough to look into my eyes.

"I want you," he says. "No games. I just want you."

SKY

I want you. No games. I just want you.

My heart pounds at the impossibility of those words. Even after what happened between us in Busan, I couldn't let myself hope that he would want more from me.

Byunho's dark, serious eyes stare into mine, waiting for an answer.

But I can't let this get to my heart. He's not saying he wants to be my boyfriend. I push his hands away from me, stepping back to put some distance between us. It's not much, but it's all that's keeping me from giving in as anger, desire, and confusion swirl inside of me.

"You just want to have sex with me," I say, translating what he really means.

He flinches slightly, his eyebrows furrowing. "Not just that," he says.

"What else, then?" I demand, though my voice is just barely above a thin, desperate whisper.

Byunho sighs, real frustration in his voice. "Your smile. Your... friendship. We don't have to do anything. Just—" He clenches his jaw, cutting himself off. "Let me drive you home," he finishes.

BYUNHO

There's something wild and unhinged inside of me right now. All I can think about is getting Sky to trust me again. I don't even fully understand why, but I need her to look at me again the same way she did before.

She swallows. "Okay."

We get back in the car. My chest feels light with relief and heavy with guilt at the same time.

"I'm sorry for how I acted after Busan," I say, eyes focused on the road as I get us back on track to Itaewon. "I needed some time."

She says, "I'm sorry for freaking out."

"No, I... Once again, I've been acting like an asshole," I admit, frustrated with myself. "I took advantage of you."

To my surprise, she laughs. "No, you didn't."

I glance over at her. "What?"

"You didn't... take advantage of me." She looks away, unable to hold my gaze. "I wanted it, too."

My hands grip the wheel tightly as my brain helpfully supplies the detailed memory of what happened that night. I shift slightly on my seat, trying to ignore the rush of blood to my dick.

"Can I ask you something?" Sky asks, seemingly oblivious to her effect on me.

I nod without looking at her.

"Have you dated a lot of women?"

The question catches me completely off guard, but at least it completely kills my arousal. "Oh, I...I haven't dated any women," I admit.

SKY

I stare at Byunho in disbelief. "Sorry? Did you just say you've never dated any women before?"

Byunho grimaces. "Yes. I've been too busy."

Horror fills me as I realize something. "Wait, are you saying you were a *virgin*?"

The idea that I could have taken Seo Byunho's virginity is so impossible that my mind can't begin make sense of it.

Registering my disbelief with a quick glance, he shakes his head. "No, I wasn't a virgin," he explains, chuckling in self-deprecation. "I've just never been in a relationship with any woman that I slept with."

Oh. I guess I'd never considered that Byunho had never been in a relationship before. Now it's my turn to feel embarrassed about assuming a man who looks like him could possibly be a virgin.

Suddenly, I remember something. "Then what about..." I shake my head, too embarrassed to ask. "Nevermind."

He frowns. "What?"

"Your dating rumor with Iseul from BADKITTY." I want to know if it's true, especially because of what Aera told me about Iseul. That she and one of Aera's former friends were responsible for Aera being sent away to the U.S., after they walked in on Hajun and Aera making out in a practice room in the middle of the night and traded the information to her father for company favor.

BYUNHO

I wince.

Iseul. Just after debut, she boldly pursued me. I was younger, naive, and she was cruel and beautiful. To be honest, we had nothing in common and it hardly mattered for a little while. She wanted my body, but laughed in my face when I asked her to be my girlfriend. Sleeping with her eventually made me hate myself.

After a clip of her whispering to me and holding my arm at an award show circulated the internet and sparked dating rumors, I tried to break it off with her. She couldn't believe anyone would ever dare to reject her. Now, whenever we see each other, it's icy glares or cold indifference from her. I know she hates me, but I'm only ashamed that I let her use me for so long.

"We hooked up, but we never dated," I admit. My face flushes with self-disgust. "I'm not proud of it. You must think I'm a bad guy."

Sky touches my arm. "No, I don't think that."

We've reached Sky's street. I put the car into park and look over at her. Her eyes are gentle, her face soft. "You're not a bad guy," she insists, her hand still on my arm.

"Sky," I murmur, glancing down at her hand on my arm.

SKY

Byunho is looking at me, his dark eyes indecipherable. I lift my hand from his arm. "Thanks for the ride," I say, but I make no move to get out of the car. I can't, not when he's looking at me like that.

I want you. No games. I just want you.

"Sky," he murmurs again. My heart skips a beat as he leans across the center console, his eyes flickering to my lips but not closing the distance.

I lean forward and brush my lips briefly against his before leaning back and saying, "You can come up with me. If you want."

His eyes narrow and he stares at me, perplexed.

My heart pounds, despite my nonchalant suggestion. "You can prove your intentions by us spending time together without having sex."

Byunho's brows draw together, a disbelieving smirk forming at the corners of his mouth. "You're testing me?"

I nod.

He smothers his bemused smirk and nods seriously. "Okay. I accept."

EIGHTEEN

> Good night, my moonlight / Come and embrace me deeply / Lying on the ripples of the embroidered night sky"
>
> — "Gold Dust," NCT 127

BYUNHO

A FEW MINUTES LATER, after I've found a place to park a couple blocks away, Sky buzzes me into her apartment building. I'm too curious to learn more about her to say no to an offer to see her space. I go up a narrow stairwell, at the top of which she stands inside the door to her apartment, sticking her head into the hall and glancing around as if someone might be spying on us. "Come on!" she whispers loudly.

I chuckle at her loud whisper, but step quickly inside as she closes the door. Immediately, I realize how small the place is, as there's just enough space for us both to stand in the narrow area behind her door. Only a few inches apart, she looks up at me as I gaze down at her.

SKY

My heart thuds against my ribs, and I realize how crazy I must have been to suggest him coming into my apartment. I clear my throat. "Let's—" I trip over a pile of my shoes and begin to fall. I grab onto the thing nearest to me, which happens to be Byunho's shirt.

Byunho seizes my arms to steady me, but I'm already falling. I pull him down with me.

As we tumble onto the floor together, my hip slams painfully into the step separating the entryway from the short hallway leading to the rest of the apartment. I land halfway on top of Byunho.

"Are you okay?" he asks immediately, concern in his voice.

"Ow. Yep." I begin to laugh, embarrassed at my clumsiness. "This is the second time you've caught me today."

"I don't mind." Byunho smirks, and my heart starts to race again as I realize how close our bodies are. Unable to maintain eye contact, I brace myself on the floor to sit up off of him. He sits up, too, trying to hide his wince.

"Did I hurt you?" I ask in alarm. My gut twinges with guilt. He has to perform tomorrow at KOSMIC's first comeback music show. "I'm so sorry."

"No, I'm fine. I'm just tired. It's normal after a performance."

"Do you... I mean, you can stay here tonight." I don't know what I was thinking when I invited him up, but clearly, I was being impulsive. We both have to work tomorrow, and it's getting late.

"Are you sure?" he asks.

"Yes." I nod, sounding surer than I feel.

"But no sex," he clarifies, raising a brow as he smirks in amusement.

I swallow. "Right." Embarrassment makes me drop his gaze, my cheeks warming. I change the subject. "The place is really small, but make yourself comfortable."

BYUNHO

Sky kicks her shoes off and pads into the apartment in her socks. I follow her lead, looking around the tiny space. The door to the bathroom is immediately to the right, and beyond that on the other side of the wall from the bathroom is the kitchen, with the stove and washing machine right next to one another and a short counter space.

"Sorry, just ignore the mess," Sky says, biting her lip as she gazes around at her surroundings, as if she's looking at them for the first time, too.

A small two-person table sits next to the wall along with two chairs. The table has various items on it, a half-full coffee mug and a pair of headphones on top of a closed laptop. On the other side of that is a large beanbag that serves as a couch, sitting beside a low table next to the window. A narrow ladder beside the bean bag must lead up to the loft bedroom.

While I look around, Sky busies herself trying to tidy the space.

Small hints of Sky's personality are everywhere, from purple and orange throw pillows on her beanbag to a row of green plants on the floor next to the window. A small shelf holds a few books and K-pop albums. I recognize KOSMIC's last album.

Smirking, I pull it out of the shelf and glance at Sky. When she glances over to see what I'm doing, she covers her mouth, looking mortified.

"Whose photo card did you get," I wonder aloud, opening the album to take a look.

"Oh my god, stop that!" Sky exclaims, lunging to grab the album from my hands. I turn away, blocking her from grabbing it. "Please! That's so embarrassing," she begs.

I chuckle at her reaction. Finding Simon's photo card inside, I glance at her sideways, frowning. "Not my photo card?"

"It's random," she mutters defensively.

I pocket the photo card. She doesn't get to keep one that's not mine. "I'll get you some of mine instead."

A jar of pens sits on top of the small shelf, so I grab one and sign my name on the album itself as Sky watches with her mouth open. Then I put the album back on the shelf.

"I can't believe you just did that," she says.

I shrug, smiling a little. The amazement on her face is priceless.

SKY

While Byunho is in my bathroom getting ready for bed, I panic.

I have no idea what I'm doing. And this man I had the most fantastic sex of my life with, who happens to be my coworker and my celebrity crush... is in my apartment right now.

I stuff my dirty laundry into the washing machine where he can't see it, then change into my pajamas.

As I'm changing, I hear Byunho walk into the living area below the ladder. "Don't look!" I squeak, even though he's literally seen all of me already. I pull my shirt on and pop my head over the railing. He's dutifully turned towards the wall, studying a macrame tapestry I made that's hanging on the wall. He's already wearing a t-shirt and shorts that he brought with him in a bag he had in his car.

"You can look now," I say. "And if you're ready for bed, um, you can just shut off the lights down there and then come up."

Byunho nods, turning to look up at me. "I can sleep down

here if you want," he offers, his brows furrowed with uncertainty.

My stomach flips with nerves. "No, I've fallen asleep on that thing before and my neck always hurts the next day. Besides... we've slept together before. I trust you."

Hesitating for another moment, Byunho goes to turn off the lights, so that the only light is the lamp at the top of the ladder to the loft.

"Watch your head," I say as he climbs up the ladder. There is only enough space between the floor and the ceiling for me to sit up, not stand, up here, and he has to duck his head to fit up here.

The small space has just enough room for my lamp, a small fan that I've turned on to keep cool, and my mattress sitting on the floor, which has a mountain of pillows and is just big enough for two people. Aera has slept over here before and we had plenty of room. Although, Byunho is a lot taller than she is.

I scoot over against the wall, making room for Byunho to climb onto the mattress.

But he doesn't.

BYUNHO

"What's wrong?" Sky asks, an edge of concern in her voice.

My chest tightens, not wanting her to worry. But I can't make myself move. The intimacy of sleeping in her bed with her... even though we've done that and more once before, it means something different now. Something more.

"Nothing, I..." I shake myself. I climb slowly onto the bed beside her.

"Are you sure?" she asks.

I look at her, and she looks so beautiful with no makeup, face glowing in the soft golden light of the lamp. In answer, I reach up to touch her face. She goes very still, eyes on mine. "Is it against the rules if I kiss you?" I ask softly.

Sky shakes her head. I lean forward and place my mouth against hers.

She exhales, winding her arms around my neck as I kiss her, taking my time to taste and caress every corner of her mouth. She shifts, pulling me down, and I lay down beside her as she presses her hips and stomach against mine. Despite my sore muscles and the dragging fatigue I feel from performing, my body can't help but respond to her touch.

I ignore my arousal. We're not doing anything more than kissing tonight.

We stay like that for a long time, lying beside each other with our mouths gently moving together, until I feel like I could forget my own name by losing myself in the sensation of her. The only sound is the whir of the fan, blowing cool air onto our flushed skin.

Finally, she puts her hand on my chest and lifts her head. "We should sleep," she whispers regretfully. "It's late."

I nod, reluctantly pulling away to reach over and turn off the lamp, darkness falling around us like a soft blanket.

Sky throws the cover over us and nestles against my body as she did before, fitting her head into the space between my head and shoulder and resting her arm across my stomach.

"Goodnight," she whispers.

My chest aches again. I've never wanted anything more badly than for her to hold me like this.

"Goodnight," I murmur, touching her arm lightly.

Exhausted and aching strangely inside and out, I fall asleep.

NINETEEN

> "Fire to the low, lower, low / Don't run away, run away, yeah / Come to the low, lower, low / Drown in you / All the way, all the way, yeah"

— "Smoke Sprite," SoYoon ft. RM

BYUNHO

"WHERE WERE YOU LAST NIGHT?" Changmin asks me early the next morning, after I arrive at the music show we're recording today. I only got here a few minutes after they did, but the members have been blowing up my phone asking where I am and I have five missed calls from Manager Sangjin. When Sangjin saw me walk through the door, he almost collapsed in relief.

Changmin's voice is calm and light, but he watches my response closely.

"I'm here now." Where I was last night is not something Changmin needs to know. Although I respect him as the band's leader, that's where I draw the line.

Sky got here before I did. We decided it would be better to arrive separately rather than risk being seen together. Because of traffic, her taking the metro was faster than my car. And right now, she's helping Haru with his stage outfit. Her eyes catch mine, and she gives me a shy smile.

Changmin turns to follow my gaze, but thankfully Sky is no longer looking in our direction, her attention turned back to Haru.

I smile to myself.

SKY

Each day of the first week of comeback promotions is packed with performances. Despite the company's worries about KOSMIC being able to make a come back after the scandal, the album becomes a top-selling new release and KOSMIC collects a respectable number of music show wins.

The tension between Byunho and I has shifted. As I'm working, I'll look over to find him watching me. When I come over to adjust his outfit or touch up his makeup or hair, he holds my gaze in a way that makes me want to squirm. Then, at one of the last music shows of the week, he slips a note into my pocket with his phone number written on it.

My stomach fluttering with nerves, I wait until after work to text him. I've just finished organizing and putting away some items at the office. I'm wearing my hair up today, with a black pencil skirt and an indigo blouse.

I hesitate over what to type.

Did you want to talk to me?

He responds almost immediately, making my pulse jump.

> Yes. Are you still at the office? Come to Floor 5. I want to show you something.

> Okay. Leaving now

My nerves have turned to full butterflies. I wave to Mrs. Goh and her daughter Miyoung, who's here again today, as I leave.

I don't spend much time upstairs in the main lobby, except to go fetch coffee from the office cafe for my coworkers. As usual, I get a couple curious looks, but nobody stops me or pays any particular attention to me as I punch the number 5 on the elevator.

When I reach Floor 5, however, I discover a problem. Like Aera's administrative office floor, there's a glass wall with a key pad next to the door blocking me and any other unqualified personnel from entering. Just as I'm about to panic, Byunho appears around the corner and opens the door for me.

"Come on," he whispers, beckoning me over.

Heart pounding, I follow him quickly around the corner, where he stops in front of a door with another keypad and punches in a code. He ushers me in first, then follows and shuts the door behind us. I hear the lock click.

The room is an office. Or I guess more accurately, a studio space. I remember seeing it in the background of some of his live broadcasts, which he does very rarely.

"My studio," he says, waving his hand across the room as he leans his shoulder against the doorframe beside me.

I take in the space. It's simple, with a black leather couch along one wall, a large bookshelf on the other side, and a desktop with studio equipment taking up the far wall, including stands holding a couple electric guitars and a keyboard.

I look at Byunho for explanation as I take a couple of steps toward the bookshelf, which holds various music related items and equipment. "Why did you bring me here?"

"You showed me your apartment, so I thought I'd show you where I spend most of my time outside of schedules." He watches me, a slight smile on his lips as I glance through his music collection, too nervous to meet his gaze. I notice the blue elephant plushie his little sister gave him sitting on the shelf closest to his desk. I gently pet its head and trunk, like it's a living animal.

"Before I forget," Byunho says, drawing my attention away from the cute elephant. He retrieves a paper envelope off the shelf and hands it to me. He seems to be trying not to smile.

"What is it?" I ask, looking inside.

It takes me a moment to figure out what I'm looking at. It's a stack of Byunho photocards.

I can't help but laugh. "Are you kidding me?"

"Did you think I'd forget?" he says, grinning.

I shake my head in disbelief. "Is that why you brought me up here?"

"No, I just missed you," he says, looking down at me with a smirk. I'm suddenly very aware of the space between our bodies. "Do you want to hear what I'm working on?" he asks.

There are two screens on his desktop, showing something technical looking which draws my attention—various lines of audio stacked on top of one another in a music program.

Excitement bubbles up in me. "Really?"

Byunho nods, smiling. He crosses the room and takes a seat at his desk chair, clicking a couple of times. Then he spins his chair around. I'm still standing in the center of the room, hesitant to move closer. "Come here," he says, tapping his thigh.

My heart jumps into my throat.

He smirks in amusement. "I'm not going to do anything to you. Come here."

I approach cautiously. Byunho seizes my waist gently and pulls me into his lap, where I perch awkwardly for a moment before settling back against his chest as he pulls me closer. Every cell of my body that touches him feels charged with an electrical current.

Reaching around me, he picks up a pair of headphones on his desk and places them over my ears, his arms on other side of me and my back leaning against his chest. Then he presses play on the computer.

A beat plays in my ears, which has an extremely catchy groove that I can't help but nod my head to. I listen closely until the end of the track, which concludes with some soft electric guitar. When it ends, Byunho takes off the headphones and sets them back on the desk.

"What do you think?" he murmurs in my ear, making me shiver.

I turn my head to look at him. His face is a mere breath from mine. "I don't know anything about producing music," I whisper. "But I love the way it sounds."

Byunho smiles. Impulsively, I lean forward and kiss him.

BYUNHO

My hand tightens on Sky's waist as I kiss her back, our mouths moving slowly together. The scent of her perfume, peach and orange blossom, is intoxicating. Her teeth graze my lower lip, and I can't help but groan. "Sky."

"Byunho," she gasps into my mouth.

Frustrated with our position, I pick her up into my arms and carry her to the couch, where I sit down with her falling back against my chest. Without missing a beat, she turns to face me, kneeling between my legs. She wraps her arms around my neck to kiss me again and presses her chest against mine. I run my hands down her sides, wishing I could grab her ass in that tight skirt, but not wanting to take it further than kissing without her consent.

Breathless, she pulls away for a moment. "Should we be doing this here?" she asks, her eyes sliding nervously over to the door.

SKY

"Door's locked. Room is soundproof," Byunho says, his voice deep and rough, sending shivers down my spine. "We can do whatever we want and no one will hear us."

I bite my lip, heart pounding wildly in my chest. "I want you."

His breath catches as he holds my gaze. "Right now?"

I nod. Byunho takes my chin in my hand and kisses me again, slowly, making my head spin. His hands start unbuttoning my blouse, exposing the lacy white bra beneath as it falls open. Then he finds the zipper on the side of my skirt and unzips it. I fumble at the laces on his sweatpants until we get them off. He produces a condom from one of his jacket pockets before tossing the jacket on the floor.

"You had one this whole time?" I demand in fake outrage.

He chuckles and kisses me again, holding the foil between his fingers but in no hurry to use it, taking his time just kissing me. He's wearing the necklace I made him. I touch each of the beads resting just above his collarbones, an indescribable emotion filling my chest.

"What about your test?" he asks in a low voice.

I shake my head. "You passed it," I say, looking into his eyes.

"So what do I get?" he asks, a smirk at the corner of his mouth as his eyes dip hungrily to my body.

BYUNHO

To my surprise, Sky takes the condom from my fingers. She reaches down, taking my hard, aching cock in her hands. She strokes the length, squeezing it gently. I close my eyes, letting out a shuddering breath at how good it feels for her to touch me. Then I open them again so I can watch her.

I can barely breathe as she opens the foil and rolls it slowly over my dick. She bites her lower lip between her teeth as she meets my eyes. "Touch me," she whispers.

She doesn't have to ask me twice. I slide my hands beneath her skirt, briefly squeezing her ass before working her panties down and off. I slide my hands back up, dipping my fingers into the wetness of her core.

She makes a little sound and leans forward to kiss me as I find and tease her clit with my fingertips, making gentle, coaxing circles around the sensitive bud as I grip her ass cheek with my other hand.

Her arms wrap around my shoulders again, putting her chest in my face. I kiss the exposed top of her breast, wetting her skin with my tongue so she gasps. She undoes her shirt more and pushes her bra down, letting her breasts spring free of their cups, smooth and brown and full. I kiss them each slowly, teasing her nipples each in turn with my tongue, sucking on them as I stroke between her legs. Her hands grip onto my hair, as I work her body until she cries out in pleasure.

Sky is breathing hard, her chest still pressed against my face. I listen to her pounding heart slow until she pulls back to look down at me. My dick throbs when she meets my eyes, lips parted, curls falling out of her ponytail to frame her face. "I need you to promise me something," she says, her pretty brown eyes filled with seriousness.

I would promise her anything right now. I nod, my crow creasing.

"Promise me you won't break my heart," she says.

My chest constricts for a moment, as if she's taken my heart in her fist and squeezed. At this moment, I know it's more likely that she'll break my heart, and I would let her. I hold her gaze. "I promise, Sky. I would never do anything to hurt you."

She smiles and leans forward to kiss me. As she does so, she places her hand on my shoulder and takes my cock in her hand, guiding me to her center. I groan as she sinks slowly onto me, her body tight around mine and so good that I can only surrender to her. She moves over me until I come apart.

TWENTY

" Inside my heart, there's nothin' but a burning flame / If you want my love / Come a little bit closer"

— "Bad Decisions," BTS ft. benny blanco & Snoop Dogg

SKY

I GO to work the next day feeling like I'm floating through a dream.

Byunho's eyes lock onto mine the moment he walks into the dressing room at the music show, and I remember my first day of work when his eyes did the same thing. I look away quickly. My cheeks are hot as I remember what we did yesterday in his studio. By the look in his eyes, it seems like he was thinking about it, too.

I busy myself with ironing a pair of pants until I feel my phone buzz in my pocket. I sneak a glance across the room to find Byunho watching me, so I pull my phone out of my pocket to check my messages.

One good thing about dating my stylist is that I
get to see you almost every day.

My eyes pop. I look up at him to find satisfied amusement
on his face.

Dating??

Yes

It's so like him to suddenly declare that. I try to smother my
grin, intoxicating giddiness filling my chest.

You better take me on a date then.

* * *

MS. GOH SAID I seem distracted. She's probably right, but the
quality of my work isn't suffering.

At least, I didn't think it was, until things start happening.

In addition to interviews and variety show appearances,
KOSMIC has numerous performances on their comeback
schedule. It means performing the same song again and again,
but with different costumes and set changes each time.

The first time something happens is during a pre-recorded
performance. A seam splits in Byunho's pants, causing them to
rip open along one thigh. He has to change pants and they have
to re-record that part.

Ms. Goh isn't happy, but she doesn't blame me for it. I think
it was just an unlucky accident until it happens to Byunho
again, a few days later, at another performance.

KOSMIC is ready to go onstage, and I'm sitting backstage
next to Eunjung and a talkative makeup artist. I try
halfheartedly to keep up with the conversation, but my attention

is on the screen monitor on the wall, where it shows their live broadcast performance.

Halfway through the song, the buttons on Byunho's jacket pop open, first one and then another.

I jump up and grab supplies, but there's nothing I can do because this performance is live. Standing by the stage exit, I watch Byunho perform with his jacket flapping open.

By the time it's over and the members are coming off stage, Stylist Goh is also there. "What happened?" she demands of me in front of the band and other staff members.

"I'm sorry," I say, staring at the floor, feeling the eyes of everyone on me.

"I didn't ask if you're sorry, I asked what happened."

"The buttons didn't hold." My throat tightens and my eyes prickle like I might start crying, but I can't let myself lose it in front of all these people.

"It was an accident," I hear Byunho say. I look up to see him addressing Stylist Goh on my behalf. "It's because I danced too aggressively."

My chest nearly cracks open with gratitude for him, but Stylist Goh stands firm.

"Even so. You as a performer work hard not to make mistakes on stage. We can't afford to make mistakes with costumes." She pins me with a needle-sharp look.

But in the end, Goh lets me live.

Back in the dressing room, I take the jacket from Byunho. He gives me a look full of silent concern, but I shake my head at him.

The buttons popped off, so I go out on the stage to look for them so I can sew them back on later. It's strange to stand on the empty stage, with all its bright lights and the quickly emptying audience. I try to ignore the fans still in the crowd who notice me and look at me with curiosity.

I swallow back the tears that want to come out of my eyes. And I work harder to prevent mistakes like that at following performances, thinking there must be something I'm doing wrong.

* * *

"HEY, BABY GIRL!"

As if sensing my gloomy mood from oceans away, my mom calls me that same night. It's like parents have a special power to sense when the worst time is to call and ask how you're doing. But I answer anyway, because I miss them.

"We haven't talked in so long! How are you?" Mom is sitting on the couch in our living room, which I recognize because of the print on the wall above her head. I'm lying on the beanbag in my apartment, where I've basically been since I got home.

"I'm fine." At the moment, I have no idea what to talk to her about.

"You sound tired. Is work going okay?"

"Work is a bit stressful. A costume I styled broke on stage, twice, so I have to deal with that."

"Oh dear. Well, I was thinking, I know you're working really hard over there, but we would love to see you for Christmas and New Year's. It seems like you could use a break, too."

"I'll think about it," I tell her. "Anyway, don't worry too much. It's not all bad."

"Oh? Do you have something to share?" Mom raises her brows.

My face heats. "It's... well, I guess, but I..."

"I knew it! You met a boy, didn't you?" Her voice is knowing.

I hear my father's disembodied voice. "She has a boyfriend in Korea?"

Mom giggles. "What's he like? Is he nice?"

"He's probably in one of those K-Pop boy bands," Papa's voice says, still off-screen.

I nearly choke in shock. But I get my voice back a moment later, interrupting their speculation.

"No, I don't have a boyfriend! Why would you just assume that without me saying anything?" I want to bang my head against the wall. "And anyway, why would you immediately assume I'm dating a celebrity? Do you think every man in Korea is in a K-Pop band? That's ridiculous."

But what's really ridiculous is that, in a million-to-one chance, my dad is actually right.

"You didn't have to say anything. I can tell by how you responded," Mom says. "There's at least someone you really like. Well, if you don't want to tell us about him right now, that's okay. But maybe you should invite him to visit with you during the holidays."

"I want to meet this guy," Papa adds.

When my parents get these ideas in their head, they're not going to let them go. "Right. Okay, so, I'm hanging up now."

"Just be safe—"

I hang up.

TWENTY-ONE

I DON'T NEED your touch / As long as it's your love / Come closer, come closer"

— "CLOSER," RM

SKY

After promotions for KOSMIC's comeback wrap up, I start working on other projects with other groups, including prep for BADKITTY's upcoming comeback. I haven't had any more mishaps with outfits since KOSMIC's activities ended, which is a relief. One Friday morning, the members of the girl group come down to the dressing room for their fitting for their music video shoot.

Mrs. Goh has me organizing the clothing racks by scene when the members walk in. Each of them is so perfect and beautiful in person, even dressed casually. I can't help but look at Iseul, who I now know was involved with Byunho at one point. The knowledge makes my stomach churn with jealousy and a futile need to compare myself to her.

She looks over at me as if she senses my gaze, and I drop my eyes, annoyed with myself for being caught staring.

"So you're the new stylist, right?" she asks me as soon as I come over to make an adjustment on her first outfit. Her lips curve as she looks me up and down. "You're from America."

"Yes," I agree politely, avoiding her gaze as I wrap a measuring tape around her tiny waist. I can feel her examining me with mild disdain, like I'm a bug on the floor.

"Hmm," she says. Whatever that's supposed to mean.

I'm not looking forward to these next couple months of working with her.

As I'm taking measurements of another member—I recognize her, but I can't remember her name—she touches my arm and smiles slightly at me. "Don't let her get to you," she says quietly.

Feeling encouraged, I smile back.

* * *

THAT EVENING as I wrap up at my workstation, I see Miyoung, Mrs. Goh's daughter. I haven't actually talked to Miyoung in a while, since before I went to Busan, but I make a point to smile at her and ask how she's doing.

She stares at me for a moment before responding. "I'm fine."

I guess she's still shy, and I can't force her to be friends with me if she doesn't want to be.

My phone dings with a message. It's Byunho.

Are we still on for tonight?

Just reading a text from him makes my stomach flutter. I smile as I type my answer.

> Sure, I should be home around 6:30!

He replies a few minutes later.

> I can be there at 7:15.

* * *

I LEAVE the office that evening with my bag slung over my shoulder, excited to go home and see Byunho later. The sun has just set, casting the district of Gangnam into shadows. As I'm walking away from the employee exit on route to the subway, a strange prickle creeps up the back of my neck.

There are people out and about, but it's not crowded. Streetlights and signs illuminate the sidewalks enough that I usually don't feel too worried about walking around at night, not like in the U.S.

Holding my breath, I look back over my shoulder.

A hooded figure is walking about a block behind me, a mask covering their face. Though it's not obvious whether they're following me, my heart stutters with fear, sure that this person is the cause of the chill I felt.

Shaken, I walk faster, glancing over my shoulder every so often, until I reach the metro. I only have to wait a few minutes for my train, but they're some of the longest moments of my life as I watch for the same figure to appear.

They don't. I breathe a long sigh of relief as I board my train.

I'm being paranoid. Something about dating an international superstar is getting to my head, making me think that I'm important enough to be stalked by someone. It was a one-time scare, just some creep following me because I'm a foreigner, maybe.

I dismiss the experience, and because of how giddy I am to see Byunho, it's shockingly easy to do.

By the time Byunho arrives at my apartment later that night, I've already forgotten about it.

BYUNHO

I know my members suspect something, because of the looks they've been giving me after I spent that night away from the dorm. When I'm texting Sky, I turn my phone so that they won't be able to see who it is I'm talking to. Knowing better than to bother me about it, they leave it alone. Suddenly, I understand why Hajun was so angry about us getting in his business about Aera.

My date with Sky is at her apartment, for lack of another place to spend time together. Being so recognizable in public means that taking her to a nice restaurant while keeping our relationship a secret is a bit challenging. However, I can still cook for her at home.

I stand outside Sky's door, carrying a bag of groceries and some flowers.

The door opens and she appears, her face lighting up when she sees the bouquet of pinkish yellow roses wrapped in brown paper and tied with string. "Shut up! You got me flowers?"

"Shut up? I didn't say anything." I chuckle and hand her the bouquet, then step through the threshold to her apartment and close the door. I pull my mask down and take my cap off, setting the bag of groceries on the narrow counter.

"These are beautiful." Sky smiles, lifting the flowers to her nose to smell them. "Thank you."

Hands now free, I grab her by the waist and pull her against me, making her squeak. I bury my face into the curls on the side of her head and inhale her sweet, floral scent.

"Are you smelling me?" she asks, giggling.

"Mm," I mumble. "How was your day?"

"It was weird," Sky says, a strange note in her voice. The lightheartedness from a moment ago is gone. I pull back to examine her face.

"Why?" I prompt, frowning. "Sit down while I cook for you." I guide her to sit down at the kitchen table before I tie my hair back and begin taking the groceries out of the bag. Tonight I'm making a simple stir fry with vegetables and sweet potato glass noodles—japchae.

"Do you want my help?" she asks.

I shake my head. "Just relax and talk to me. How was your day weird?"

Sky sighs. "It seems like nothing is going right at work lately. There haven't been any other problems with outfits since the comeback promotions for you guys ended, but now that we're working on BADKITTY's comeback... Iseul is there, and she's just awful. I can only imagine what she would do if she knew I was dating you."

I wince, and not only because the onions I'm chopping sting my eyes. "I'm sorry."

She hesitates before saying, "I guess I still don't understand why you would be with her if she didn't treat you well... when you could have anyone you wanted."

I frown, wishing I didn't have to talk about this. But all I can do is be truthful to Sky now. "When I came to Seoul, I wasn't happy. Even after we debuted... it took us so long to finally debut. I wasn't happy, and Iseul knew how to take advantage of that," I explain. "Not that it excuses me from acting the way I have in the past. But I don't want to be a selfish, cruel person like her."

Sky absorbs this for a moment. "I don't understand why you say things like that. You're amazing."

My heart eases a little, and I flash her a grateful smile. But I know that sooner or later, I'm going to have to tell her about my past.

TWENTY-TWO

> That moonlight that shines on me at dawn / It's still the same as then / A lot changed in my life, but / That moonlight is still the same"

— "Moonlight," Agust D

SKY

THE HEAT of summer fades quickly, and the leaves on the trees begin to burn golden and red. Busan was only a couple of months ago, and yet so much has changed.

KOSMIC is busy preparing for their world tour, the first concert to take place in Seoul in only a few weeks. Byunho texts me every day and comes to my apartment whenever he can get away, which sometimes just means to eat and sleep. We can't go out in public, with his face being so recognizable.

The fact remains that I can't tell anyone about me and Byunho. Not my mom or dad. Not even Aera, even though I know she would understand.

On our regular brunch date, Aera tells me about meeting

the real estate agent for the villa she and Hajun are purchasing together, and the agent's judgmental attitude about the fact that Hajun and Aera aren't married.

"I don't understand why living together is such a big deal. People already know you and Hajun were a thing," I comment, nibbling on a macaron as I try to explain my thinking. "Like, the public doesn't know you're back together, but it's not like moving in together is weird for a couple." People live together all the time without being married, so I'm missing something about why it's somehow wrong for her and Hajun to get a place together.

The soft background of cafe noise covers our quiet conversation, and thankfully there's no one sitting very close to us.

"It's because of status and reputation," Aera explains. "Living together as an unmarried couple... that's not done by people like me."

Right. Chaebol heiress and all.

"But if I told my dad abba about wanting to be with Hajun seriously, he could punish him, remove him from the company for good— I can't do that to him."

I think about what could happen to Byunho's career if anyone found out about our relationship, and I set down the cookie I was about to eat, no longer hungry.

"So you're still going to keep it secret?" I ask, hopelessness curdling my stomach. "How? What about that bodyguard your dad has follow you around sometimes?" I look over at the opposite corner of the cafe, where her bodyguard sits sipping a coffee.

"I'm going to rent a smaller place in an adjacent complex that shares the same parking structure. For all anyone else will know, I'm just moving out on my own."

"Ha. Can I sublet? Nevermind, I probably can't afford it." I wince, thinking with an inward shudder about the cockroach that got into my apartment and which Byunho killed for me last week. I take a sip of my pumpkin spice latte, trying to forget about how I shrieked loudly when I saw it and Byunho laughed at me.

"Sure," Aera agrees easily, teasing me. "I'll give you a best friend discount. Your current place in Itaewon is too far for your commute, anyway." She seems to be seriously considering it.

"No, I was joking! I can't let you pay my rent!" I throw my hands up. After all of the things that Aera has done for me and thinks nothing of, the only things I have to give back are love and loyalty, which are things I would give her anyway.

Aera gets a thoughtful look in her eyes that I don't like. "Why not?" she muses. "You can be my cover for living with Hajun. You'd be helping me."

BYUNHO

"I'm moving to a new apartment," Sky tells me over the phone one night. I'm in my dorm bedroom and Tai is taking a shower, which means I have a rare private moment to talk on the phone with her instead of just texting.

"Why? Is it because of the cockroach?" I ask, thinking back to last week when she was cleaning her apartment while I was cooking us dinner. A cockroach scurried out from behind some furniture. She shrieked and climbed up on a chair, while I cornered and killed it. It wasn't a big deal to me, but her reaction was funny.

"No, it's not that," she says with an embarrassed huff. "I'm actually trying to do Aera a favor. She needs a roommate for this apartment, but she won't really be living there. It's complicated. But I need to move out this weekend so that I don't have to pay next month's rent for my current apartment—I already checked with the landlord. Aera is out of the country on a business trip right now, but I'm allowed to move in to the new place next weekend."

I process this information for a moment. "Where is this new apartment?"

"In Samseong-dong. Which makes my commute a lot shorter... and you'll be closer, too." I can practically hear her blushing, which makes me smile.

"I'll help you move," I say.

"You don't have to do that." She still tries to refuse letting me buy things for her or do anything for her.

"I want to."

Realizing she can't argue with me, Sky relents. "Okay, but can you get away this weekend?"

"I can," I promise, just as the door opens, and Tai comes into the bedroom, wearing a towel around his waist.

"I need to go," I say in Korean, to disguise the fact that I was speaking in English a moment before, then hang up. Sky knows that I have to be careful about phone calls around my bandmates.

Though he gives me an assessing look, Tai doesn't ask any questions.

* * *

"YOU CHANGED YOUR HAIR!" Sky exclaims when she lets me into her apartment on Saturday. Her fingers brush the side of my face as she takes my cap off to run her fingers through my freshly cut and dyed hair.

I chuckle and lean down to kiss her. I'd gone to an appointment with my hair stylist yesterday and had him cut it shorter. We compromised on the color, and he dyed it a less conspicuous dark reddish-brown. This is the color that it's going to be for at least the first leg of our world tour.

"Sorry," I say against her lips. "I didn't realize you liked the long hair so much."

"It looks good like this too, though," she says.

Her tiny apartment is full of boxes, though thankfully she doesn't have a lot of stuff. Putting my mask and cap back on as a disguise, I start carrying her furniture down to the van. The furniture is only challenging because of the narrow stairwell, which is why, Sky huffs as we lug the beanbag down them, she never get a couch.

Next, we carry the boxes. I make a point to grab the heaviest ones before she does. "Are you sure this was what you wanted to do on your day off?" Sky questions, making me laugh. I laugh so much more often when I'm with her.

The large van is able to fit all of Sky's belongings, and I drive us to the address in Samseong where the apartment complex is. Sky has to use a key card, which she says Aera gave her, to get into the parking garage.

Leaving the van in the parking garage, we take the elevator up to the apartment.

SKY

"This is the first time I'm seeing it," I say, feeling excited and nervous as we ride the shiny metal elevator up. The parking garage was filled with nice cars, which makes me feel even more out of place.

On the eighth floor, we get off the elevator and walk down a hallway with pristine white floors until we find the number of the apartment. I use my key card again, and open the door into a large room with wood floors. When we step into the living room, we're greeted by large windows with a view of green trees and the silvery-blue river.

"Wow." I think I repeat this several times as we look around. Byunho and I explore together, going from room to room and checking out the appliances, cupboards, and closets. It's a good-sized apartment, with the living room, kitchen, and dining area sharing the same space, plus two bedrooms with a big bathroom. It's so nice that I actually can't believe that I'm going to live here.

Byunho whistles softly. "So let me get this straight. Aera is paying for you to live here so that you can claim to be her roommate, while she secretly moves in with Hajun."

I stare at him in surprise. "How did you figure that out?"

He chuckles. "Because I'm not an idiot."

I roll my eyes. So much for keeping my friend's secrets.

* * *

IT TAKES us the next few hours to move the rest of my things into the apartment. It would have taken me a lot longer if it hadn't been for Byunho's help.

While he goes to drop off the moving van with the rental company and pick up his own car, I allow myself to process how I'm feeling. There's no way I could ever afford to live in a place like this if it was just me paying for it.

Byunho comes back with takeout and after eating, we sit on the bean bag in the mostly empty living room, watching the traffic along the river in comfortable silence. I lean my head on his shoulder and let out a breath. "I'm not sure I'll get used to it, but I definitely can't complain," I finally admit. "I just feel like I don't deserve all of this."

He turns his head to look down at my head on his shoulder. "Why? Because you weren't born rich?"

I lift my head to stare at him in confusion. "What?"

"You think you don't deserve this because you don't have the money that Kim Aera has, but she was born wealthy," he explains.

"Yeah," I say slowly, "but she helped me get this job and is helping me pay for this apartment. Most people wouldn't do that."

"Maybe not," Byunho agrees. "But you work hard, too. Trust me, I know what it's like to feel like you don't deserve... all of this." He looks out toward the city, with all its buildings sparkling in the evening sunlight.

"But you're someone important," I argue. "You're a celebrity. I'm just your...stylist." And not even a good one, since I kept messing up his stage costumes.

BYUNHO

I can't help but snort in disbelief at Sky's assumption. Frustration building inside of me, I get up and pace toward the window, then turn back to meet Sky's confused gaze. "Is that all you think you are?"

Her brown eyes are wide. She seems at a loss for words.

"The only reason I'm famous, that I have money, is because I got lucky," I explain, needing her to understand. "There are plenty of people who are more talented, who worked harder, and never reached the same level of so-called success that I have. It's all an illusion, Sky. None of this"—I gesture to the city shining outside the window—"is real. I'm hardly even real." I laugh darkly.

Sky shakes her head, looking concerned now. "What do you mean, you're not real?"

I close the distance between us and kneel beside her so that we're eye to eye. "I'm not special, Sky. Even if what everyone else sees is this perfect idol, that's all fabricated. We're just people. You need to realize that and stop thinking that you don't deserve me. In reality, I probably don't deserve you." I take her hand.

Her eyes shine with tears. She pulls me toward her, and I let her. The bean bag shifts beneath us and I fall almost on top of her, which makes her laugh. Her laughter draws a smile out of me, and I kiss her gently

"I want to tell you a story about myself," I say. The sun is setting now, painting the sky with red, orange, and purple.

SKY

The seriousness in Byunho's voice makes me realize he's about to tell me something important. I sit up and fold my hands in my lap, giving him my full attention.

There's a distant look in his eyes, as if he's looking into the past. "I'm telling you this because I want you to understand that I'm not the person the world sees me as. I haven't told this whole story to anyone before."

I nod.

"When I was fourteen, my parents got divorced. My father was an alcoholic. He would yell at us and punch holes in the walls instead of hitting us. The restaurant was his and my mom's restaurant that they started together, before it was a fried chicken place." His voice is matter-of-fact, as if telling this story isn't painful for him at all. But I know it has to be.

"He let my mother have the restaurant when they divorced. My mom got remarried. My stepdad was a harsh man, always annoyed at my presence, because I was a reminder of my mother's past marriage. He criticized me constantly. I tried not to bother anyone and would spend most of my time in my room working on music, working in the restaurant, or at school. I would still visit my dad as much as possible, and give him money from my delivery job to help him pay his rent. He was really struggling. Then, when I was 16, he... took his own life."

My stomach drops.

BYUNHO

The memories flash before my eyes.

How one day when I was studying after school, my phone rang. It was my mother. She told me my father was dead.

I rode my motorbike to the hospital to see his body. After that, I took the role as the chief mourner for two nights and three days at the funeral hall in the hospital, wearing a black hanbok. I barely ate and only slept for a few hours every night.

"My stepdad prevented my mother and Hyunjoo from attending the funeral. Then, when I returned home, I couldn't go to school, no matter how much my mother begged. I didn't leave my room, and I started drinking." Sky's eyes are wide with sympathy, but she doesn't interrupt, listening to my story.

"Every time I appeared in his view, my stepdad would call me a good-for-nothing like my father. I couldn't take his abuse anymore, so when he decided to yell at me about something, I don't even remember what, I punched him."

I chuckle humorlessly. "He needed stitches. He also threw me out, of course. After that, I had no choice but to take my chances on music because I had dropped out of school. So I moved to Seoul by myself," I finish, feeling something ease in my chest after telling the story.

Sky lets out a ragged breath, her eyes full of tears, and she takes my hand in hers and holds it. "I'm so sorry that happened to you. That must be extremely painful."

I shake my head. "I didn't tell you that because I wanted pity. I just wanted you to know that I'm far from perfect. I don't always feel like I deserve the success I've had, either. And... you matter to me, Sky. You brought happiness back into my life. I had forgotten what it felt like."

SKY

"You matter so much to me, too," I say, emotions filling my chest. I move closer to him and wrap my arms around him, hugging him tight as he presses his face into my hair.

It's at that moment that I understand that there's no turning back. The feelings that I have for him are so much deeper than the celebrity crush I had on him for years, that it feels as if that was an entirely different person. I'm in love with this incredibly strong, beautiful man.

TWENTY-THREE

> "We keep all the party in this room all night / We don't wanna put it on the brake, hold tight"

— "All Night," BTS ft. Juice WRLD

SKY

AT WORK SEVERAL DAYS LATER, while Aera is still on her business trip, a representative from the PR department calls me and Ms. Goh into a meeting upstairs. "Some sort of publicity thing," my supervisor sighs.

"Why do they want to see me?" I ask her, anxiety bubbling in my stomach.

She only shakes her head. At lunch, I excuse myself into the bathroom and text Byunho:

> I'm being asked to go to a meeting with the PR department in 20 minutes. I don't know what it's about yet.

He doesn't reply, which only increases my sense of

apprehension. I can't help but think that our relationship has finally been discovered, and I'm about to be fired from my job. I text Aera, too, but she also doesn't reply.

My heart hammers from the elevator ride up to the moment we sit down in the meeting room with the representative in his dark suit and tie. I focus on trying to breathe evenly.

"I have a proposal for you," the PR representative says to Ms. Goh, before looking at me. "My team thinks it would be a great idea to showcase having an American stylist on CKM's styling team. Seoul Fashion Week is next week, and we think Ms. Flores should attend with several of our idols."

My jaw drops open. I shut my mouth quickly, swallowing a mixture of relief and disbelief.

"You would have a brief interview with a journalist, and sit with some of the idols in the audience for one of the shows. That's all that would be required of you, but I hope you will consider this a very exciting opportunity, and of course, you'll be paid," the suit finishes.

Ms. Goh turns to me. "Do you feel like you can handle this?" she asks me seriously.

It takes me a moment to find my voice. "Yes," I respond. "I can handle it."

"Great. We don't have long to prepare you, but you will need media training and appropriate attire. Ms. Goh, if you can provide the attire, I can block Ms. Flores in for media training tomorrow."

After scheduling my media training, Ms. Goh and I return downstairs. Ever since the accidents with the wardrobe malfunctions, Ms. Goh has been even colder with me. But now, she just sighs and tells me, "It is a big part of our job to manage the public image of idols and the company. It seems like more trouble than it's worth, but I know you will do a good job."

With that strangely reassuring statement, we go back to our day's work.

While I was upstairs, Byunho responded to my text about the mystery meeting with the PR department:

Tell me when you know.

I text back quickly, holding my phone close to my chest so that no one walking past me at my desk can get a glimpse of the screen.

I'm going to Seoul Fashion Week!

His reply comes a moment later:

What a coincidence. So am I.

Which means that Byunho and I are going to a public event together.

As if reading my mind before I can share my concerns, he texts:

It'll be fine. I'm a good actor

But I'm not!!!

I put my phone back in the drawer of my desk and rub my temples.

BYUNHO

Late that night, I go to Sky's new apartment, bringing a bag of groceries with me even though it's well past dinnertime. It's much easier to visit her secretly now, as I don't have to take the subway or struggle to find a good parking spot—I can simply park in one of the guest spaces in the complex's parking garage.

She lets me inside and shuts the door behind me, then looks up at me. "Thanks for coming over," she says. "I can't stop thinking about Seoul Fashion Week. Also, you didn't have to bring food."

I chuckle and lean forward to kiss her forehead. "It's the least I can do."

We put the groceries away in the kitchen, then each have a bowl of ramyun while sitting on the floor next to the windows and the glittering lights of Seoul at night.

"I'm worried about giving an interview to the press. The company is giving me a script to memorize," Sky says, setting down her bowl and chopsticks, finally finished with her noodles. "But I've never done any sort of public interview even in English, and now I have to do one in Korean. What if I mess up?" She laughs self-consciously. "How do you do this every day?"

"I don't like giving interviews in English, either," I admit. "It's uncomfortable."

"But you speak in English with me all the time," she points out. "Is that uncomfortable for you?"

"That's different." I move closer to her, smirking as I pull her suddenly onto my lap, making her shriek with surprised laughter. "I enjoy talking to you. And doing other things with you." I brush my lips against hers, teasing them open with my tongue.

Her hand seizes my shirt and tightens on the fabric. I tease her for a while longer, until she pulls away and whispers, "You're going to stay here with me tonight, right? It's hard to sleep here by myself."

I smile. "All night, babe." I intend to help her forget all her anxiety about Seoul Fashion Week.

SKY

This "babe" nickname is new. I feel my cheeks heat with pleasure.

Byunho scoops me up and carries me into the bedroom, laying me down on the bed and kissing my neck. We undress each other slowly, my body melting under his gentle touches. "We need to get you a bigger bed," he says casually, as he helps slide my underwear down my legs and off, then lowers his face between my thighs.

I gasp as his tongue strokes me, and it isn't long before I'm grinding against his face and seeing stars. Satisfied, he sits up. "Turn around, babe," he murmurs.

Without hesitation, I flip over onto my stomach. Byunho slaps my ass, making me yelp in surprise. "Good girl," he says with a chuckle, and massages my stinging flesh with one hand as I hear him tear open a condom with his teeth.

A moment later, he pulls my hips up and toward him, positioning himself behind me. I pant with anticipation as I feel the head of his cock nudge against my opening, my thighs slipping against each other from the wetness between them. He pushes into me, and I moan at how good it feels. His hands tighten on my hips as he begins thrusting slowly into me.

I push back against him, wanting more, and feel a rush of satisfaction as his breath catches and he curses under his breath. He increases his pace until all I can do is take it, as stars begin to swim in my vision once again, pleasure slamming into me all at once. I cry out, but Byunho doesn't stop.

As the pleasure fades and my senses return to me, I hear a distant echo from the next room that sounds like the front door closing. "Sky?" calls a feminine voice. Byunho and I both freeze.

"Oh shit," I say, realizing that Aera is here. "Aera got back from her business trip," I explain to Byunho. He pulls out of me reluctantly with a suppressed groan. I sit up quickly and wave toward the closet. "Hide in there," I whisper urgently. He grabs his jeans from the floor before disappearing into the walk-in closet.

Panic pounding in my veins, I quickly grab the nearest item of clothing, Byunho's sweatshirt, and put it on along with my sweatpants, before rushing into the hallway.

Aera leans against the counter in the kitchen, drinking a glass of water. "I'm sorry, did I wake you up?" she asks. "I just got back from my trip and didn't want to go home yet."

I shake my head. "No, not at all. I wasn't expecting you," I say, my voice still breathless. My hair must also look like a mess, because Aera's eyebrows rise.

"Is someone here?" she asks suspiciously, glancing at the two bowls of noodles still on the floor beside the window.

Too quickly, I blurt, "No."

"Really? Then whose sweatshirt is that?" She points at the sweatshirt I'm wearing that is clearly too big for me.

"It's mine," says a voice behind me.

Aera and I both turn in surprise to see Byunho emerging from the hallway, barefoot and shirtless, wearing only a pair of jeans. He looks at Aera with a distinctly grumpy expression.

"Um," I say.

Aera stares at him for just a moment before turning to me. "Oh," she says.

"Yeah," I admit. Another beat of silence passes. "So, um, do you want some ramyun?" I ask.

BYUNHO

"So you've been dating in secret for months," Aera says, absorbing Sky's story after she's finished telling it. We all sit together in the living area.

Sky nods, looking at me for reassurance.

"I asked Sky to keep it secret from everyone," I explain. "She didn't tell you because I asked her not to."

"So why did you change your mind?" Sky grumbles.

"You told me to hide in the closet," I say.

Aera nods slowly, trying not to smile. "I understand why you kept it secret. And I'm sorry for interrupting you." Sky coughs in embarrassment. "But you can trust me, of course." Aera gives me a look that says the feeling isn't quite mutual, which is fine. We don't really know each other, and I don't trust her entirely, either. "Also, I'm sorry for showing up unannounced. I just got back from my trip and I didn't want to go back to my father's house yet." A smile touches the heiress's usually reserved expression with warmth. "It wasn't a business trip. Hajun brought me to the Maldives."

"The Maldives?" Sky repeats excitedly.

"He implied that the whole thing was for work, but it wasn't. At all. I mean, it was suspicious to begin with, but..." Aera laughs.

Sky stares at her with suspicion. "What aren't you saying?"

Aera glances at me. "I wasn't expecting to share this news so soon, but Hajun said he would tell the members tomorrow, so you would find out anyway."

"What? What is it?" Sky demands.

"He proposed to me. We're getting married in the spring," she says, smiling widely now.

Sky jumps to her feet and tackles her friend in a hug. "That's amazing! I'm so happy for you!"

Despite myself, I find myself smiling. Sky's happiness is infectious. And I know Hajun must be happy, too.

When Sky has finally calmed down, she catches Aera up with her own news—her public appearance at Seoul Fashion Week in only a few days. "It's a good publicity tactic," Aera says. "But you're allowed to say no if you don't want to go, Sky."

"I do want to go," Sky admits. "I'm just nervous. Byunho's going, too, though."

I nod. "Along with Changmin and Jaesung."

Aera rubs Sky's arm reassuringly. "You'll do great, I know you will." She smiles. "But it's late. I'll head home." She stands, glancing at me. "I want you both to know that your secret is safe with me. And if there's anything at all I can do for both of you, let me know."

With that, the CKM Heiress leaves.

SKY

After the door shuts behind Aera, I look at Byunho and burst out laughing. "At least now she knows, and we won't have to sneak around anymore."

Byunho gazes at me for a moment, then says with amusement, "At least she didn't get me fired for daring to try something with you."

I realize he must have heard her threat when I was on the phone with Aera in the car to Busan. I cover my face in embarrassment. "I'm sorry about that. Obviously she didn't mean it."

He chuckles and pulls me close. "Do you want to go back to bed and show me how sorry you are?"

I make a sound of outrage and slap his chest, but my stomach flutters as he leans in to kiss me.

TWENTY-FOUR

" Lights, camera, action"

— "Vogue," OH MY GIRL

SKY

A DAY before I'm attending Seoul Fashion Week, Ms. Goh pulls me aside at work. "Follow me," she says, and brings me to a clocking rack.

My supervisor takes a hanger off the rack with a dress and holds it up. "I ordered this for you. It's your size," she says, pushing it into my hands.

I stand, frozen. "What?"

"For the fashion show," she says impatiently. "Go try it on now."

Goh also got me a pair of shoes and a blazer to wear with it. Because I'm bigger than most female idols whose clothes we keep in our warehouse, she had to order new items.

Each item is designer. Although seemingly specifically

selected to make me blend in, in shades of black and tan, I can tell by the quality how expensive each item is when I put them on. Goh gives me a simple designer bag to complete the look.

For some reason, I feel oddly touched.

* * *

IN PREPARATION for the public appearance, I spend hours after work braiding my hair.

On the day of the show, I spend another few hours at home doing makeup. Then I head to the office to change into my outfit, before I'm supposed to meet up with the managers and idols to ride to the show at the Design Plaza.

Even if I wanted to back out now, I can't.

At the office, as I take my dress off of the clothing rack, something catches my eye. There's a piece of paper pinned to the front of it with a safety pin. Maybe a note Ms. Goh left for me?

I unpin it and lift it up to the light. There's handwriting on it in Korean, written in dark ink. Three sentences.

> I know your secret.
> Stay away from Byunho.
> Or I will tell everyone.

My blood runs cold.

BYUNHO

"Where is she?" asks Sangjin, checking his watch impatiently.

Changmin, Jaesung, and I sit in the back of the limousine in awkward silence. Across from us sit BADKITTY's manager and none other than Han Iseul herself, plus one other member of her group.

When we met them ten minutes ago, I was unhappily surprised. Of course my ex-girlfriend would be here. Since then, I've been sitting in silence, avoiding eye contact with her.

Iseul sighs. "I don't understand, can't we just go without her? Isn't she just a stylist?"

Her manager, apparently used to appeasing Iseul, explains patiently that it's an important piece of publicity that the stylist Sky Flores come with us.

But even I have to wonder where she is. It's not like Sky to be even five minutes late for something this important.

A moment later, the elevator across the hall dings, and Sky steps out.

She looks beautiful, wearing a black dress and a tan blazer and heels, and carrying a black bag. Her dark hair flows in neat braids around her shoulders, and her makeup is flawless.

But I know instantly that something is wrong.

"Sorry I'm late," she says in Korean, bowing slightly to Manager Sangjin as he opens the door for her. Her face is tight and pale beneath her makeup.

"I'm so happy you're going with us," Jaesung tells her as the limo pulls out of the CKM building's parking garage.

"This VIP treatment must be unfamiliar for you," Iseul remarks, smiling.

I turn a sharp glare on her, which only makes Iseul smile more, having finally caught my attention.

Sky notices Iseul at that moment, and her back stiffens. Jaesung and Changmin are the only ones who attempt to ease the tension by making conversation on the way to the venue. I don't dare say anything to Sky, in case I give something away in front of Iseul. Changmin slides me a concerned look but makes no comment.

Sky answers Jaesung when he speaks to her, but otherwise is pale and silent. It's beyond frustrating not to be able to openly ask her what's wrong. My body feels tense, as if I could fight whatever is upsetting her.

We arrive at the red carpet. Iseul is the first to get out, cheers and camera flashes greeting her. Then it's her bandmate, Changmin, Jaesung, and then me. I chance one more glance at Sky's anxious face before stepping out of the limo. Sky won't be walking on the red carpet with us.

Cameras flash as we walk down the red carpet. I pose automatically with my bandmates, ignoring Iseul when she tries to stand next to me for a photo.

SKY

The driver brings us to the parking area, and Sangjin and I go in a back entrance, splitting up with BADKITTY's manager. "You're the stylist who went to Busan with Byunho, right?" he asks me in English.

I nod. "Yes."

Sangjin gives me an assessing look. "You have your invitation card, right?"

"Yes."

He talks to a guard, showing his ID, which the guard checks on a list. After we get inside, we enter a busy hallway.

Sangjin leads me back to the red carpet the long way, so that I can complete my scheduled interview with one of the journalists there. The mysterious note is burning a hole in my purse and in my mind. I adjust the strap on my shoulder. As we walk down the hall, I pass by major celebrities and feel even more unbalanced and out of place.

I don't know if I should show Byunho the note.

I don't know what I should do.

The journalist greets me, her name flying out of my head as soon as she tells me. I feel unbalanced, completely lost. Her cameraman points his camera at me, and I numbly recite my script in response to her questions.

Afterward, they take a few photographs of me with the Design Plaza building in the background.

When it's over, Sangjin tells me, "You did good." But I'm not so sure. He takes me to the runway to watch the show, which is starting soon. The lights are dim inside the large room with rows of chairs arranged around the catwalk. The idols are sitting in the first row. My seat is on the end of the row, right next to Byunho.

BYUNHO

I took Jaesung's seat next to Sky's, before he could protest. When she finally sits down beside me, it takes everything I have not to speak to her until the show starts. When the music is turned up and the models start strutting down the catwalk, it's finally safe to talk.

"Are you okay?" I ask in a low voice.

She nods, but the movement is jerky, and she doesn't meet my eyes.

My hand twitches toward her, wishing I could hold her hand, but I stop myself. Too many cameras.

We don't talk throughout most of the show, while models stride up and down the catwalk wearing various designer fashion. Sky doesn't seem to enjoy herself, and so I don't, either. Frustration bubbles up inside of me that there is something wrong I don't know how to fix.

Finally, the day's show ends. The rest of the time is for socializing and networking.

"Do you want to leave early?" I ask Sky under my breath as

we get up from our seats. She nods, relief making her shoulders sag for a moment.

So I call Sangjin and get him to arrange a ride for us.

"You're leaving now?" Jaesung asks. Changmin glances between me and Sky. Iseul watches us with interest. I don't give a fuck.

"I don't feel well," Sky says, providing an explanation that is still insufficient for me leaving with her.

Sangjin is waiting for us in a private loading area with the company car and driver he must have called. "What happened?" he asks me.

"She's not feeling well. I'm going to take her home."

Sangjin stares at me for a moment. "Okay."

I hold my hand above Sky's head to guard her from hitting it on the door jamb as she ducks inside the car.

SKY

"Tell me what's wrong," Byunho says in English, as soon as we're in the car and moving.

I glance at the driver. He doesn't seem to be listening. "I... it's true, I don't feel well," I say.

Byunho lets out a long breath, and I can feel the frustration in him. "Is this about Iseul being there?"

I shake my head.

"I can't help you if you don't tell me."

"I know." Tears prick my eyes. I consider showing him the note, still inside my purse.

I know your secret.
Stay away from Byunho.
Or I will tell everyone.

There's been no space or time to think about what this message means since I found it, but now he and I are alone.

"I found something strange," I whisper, pulling the written message from my purse and passing it to him. He unfolds it and reads it, his brow furrowed. "Someone pinned this note to my dress," I explain.

Byunho curses. Then he presses the button that rolls up the partition between us and the driver, making our conversation private. When he finally turns his gaze back to me, his gaze is dark and hard. "Where was it?"

"On a rack in the styling department."

Only CKM employees have access to the styling department. And only those who work at the styling department would know that this dress was meant for me.

"Can you think of anyone who would do this?" he asks.

The styling department narrows it down to about twenty people, but nobody there seems capable of a threat like this.

I shake my head.

Byunho curses again.

We have no way of knowing right now exactly who left the note for me. It also wouldn't help to report the note, because that would be as good as admitting that Byunho and I are dating.

Puzzle pieces click together in my mind. "Wait, there's something else," I say. I recount to him the story of how I was followed from the CKM office building to the metro after working late one evening.

"Why didn't you tell me about this?" Byunho is clenching his jaw hard, making the muscles in it jump.

"I didn't think it meant anything," I say. "I didn't want you to worry."

His eyes flash. "You were wrong for hiding that from me," he says. "Promise me you won't do it again."

I nod, something in my chest easing slightly. "I promise."

"I think you should take a vacation. It's too dangerous for you to keep working at CKM right now," he says, voice grim.

My mouth drops open. "No, I can't do that! I haven't been working for long enough to take a vacation. I could lose my job if I don't work." And I really want this job. I can't give it up now.

Byunho sighs, clearly frustrated. "Your safety is more important than this job," he reminds me.

A chill goes through me at the idea that I could actually be in physical danger from something like this.

And yet, I don't think that whoever did this would willingly reveal themselves. Which means they're unlikely to try to hurt me.

"But I think, if I investigate at work, I could find out who did it," I suggest.

"Sky," he says, warning in his voice.

"Please, just trust me."

After a long moment, he sighs again. "Fine. But don't take any risks. Don't go anywhere alone until we catch whoever did this."

"And until then, we should keep our distance from each other," I add, my heart giving a sharp pang at the idea.

He gives me a long, lingering look, as if memorizing my features in this moment, before he finally nods, agreeing to my plan.

BYUNHO

I can't sleep that night. My mind whirls, regret and anger making my body restless. No matter how I look at it, it's my fault that Sky is being threatened.

It's my fault because I pursued her and asked her to be my girlfriend. And now there's someone out there stalking her.

When I got home, I went straight to the bedroom and shut the door. To their credit, my members didn't try to talk to me about Sky. But someone must have told Tai something, because he gives me space, and doesn't complain when he hears me tossing and turning late that night.

Maybe I should go to CKM management. Dating is no longer prohibited, but there is the issue that Sky is also an employee. That could get her fired.

But there is at least one person who would be on mine and Sky's side.

* * *

"YOU WANTED TO MEET WITH ME?" Kim Aera asks the next day, closing the door to her office to give us privacy. She gestures for me to take a seat in front of her desk, then takes her seat behind it. The city shines behind her through floor-to-ceiling glass windows. A plaque on the desk displays her name, and beneath it, "Chief Operations Officer."

The atmosphere is slightly awkward, since the last time we interacted was after she walked in on me and Sky at the new apartment, and I found out that she is marrying my ex-bandmate. But this is more important than whatever awkwardness exists between us.

"It's about Sky," I say. I explain what happened with the note and the person who followed Sky one night. Aera gets up from her desk to pace in front of the window as she thinks it over.

"Thank you for trusting me with this," she says, meeting my gaze. "I'm going to quietly investigate, without filing an official report. We can't give this person any reason to follow through with their threat and go public, which means we need to keep the investigation discreet."

Some of the tension in my shoulders eases a little.

"Thank you." I stand to go, but something stops me. "I'm sorry... for how I acted when the scandal with Hajun happened. I didn't understand. But... I do now."

Aera smiles. "I know."

TWENTY-FIVE

 "Like tonight's your birthday / Every second, every minute, make me wanna celebrate it"

— "Birthday," TEN

SKY

AT WORK THAT WEEK, I'm swept away by the normal business of things. The fact that I was a guest at a day of Seoul Fashion Week doesn't mean anything to anyone. I'm still another cog in the fast-running machine of the styling department.

I examine each of my coworkers, wondering, *Could they have left the note?* Fear curls up permanently inside my belly, making me jumpy and paranoid. Eunjung putting her hand on my shoulder to get my attention is enough to make me yelp with alarm. She watches me with concern for the rest of the day, and keeps asking if I'm okay.

A week later, and still no clues are revealed. Nothing happens. Byunho and I haven't seen each other since the day at

Seoul Fashion Week. It's like I imagined the note, even though I know it's real.

Byunho's birthday is tomorrow, and I don't know how we can make plans with this threat looming over our heads.

As I'm sitting at my work station, using a sewing machine, my phone starts buzzing from inside my desk drawer. I pick up my phone and walk away from the work stations so I won't be overheard, looking at the strange number lighting up the screen. With apprehension tightening my chest, I slide to answer the call.

Changmin's voice speaks into my ear. "Hey, Sky. Do you have a minute to talk?"

Surprised because he's never called me and I don't know how he got my number, it takes me a moment to say, "Um, yeah. What's going on? Also, how did you get my number?"

"Hajun got it from Aera," he says. I can hear the smile in his voice. "The members and I are having a small party for Byunho's birthday tomorrow at our dorm and we wanted to invite you."

I'm surprised again. "Me?" It's not usual for an idol to invite a staff member to a private party. He couldn't know about mine and Byunho's relationship, could he? But it's possible that the way Byunho and I acted together at Seoul Fashion Week gave us away to everyone who knows Byunho.

"Will you come? There will be a cake," Changmin says enticingly, knowing how much I like sweet things.

For a long moment, indecision wars inside me. On the one hand, I want to say yes and attend Byunho's birthday, but on the other, I know the risk that I'm taking.

As if sensing my hesitation but not the reason for it, Changmin says, "I can pick you up from your apartment and sneak you in through our private entrance. It's not hard to do."

I sigh. What is the point of living in fear? I can't miss something as important as Byunho's birthday. "Okay, I'm in."

BYUNHO

We're no closer to finding out who left Sky that note, and we've only been able to text each other since that day at Seoul Fashion Week. I haven't seen her once since that day, and it's killing me.

A few days ago, Changmin confronted me, following me to the bathroom after practice. As I was washing my hands, he asked, "Are you dating Sky?"

My guard went up. "That's none of your business."

"You can trust me. I'm not going to talk you out of it, I know that won't go anywhere," Changmin said, in his annoyingly calm, persuasive way.

I nodded, meeting his gaze in the mirror. We'd known each other for a long time, and I did trust him. "We are." That was all there was to say about it.

SKY

It feels totally surreal, and kind of illegal, for me to be visiting the KOSMIC members' dorm. Changmin holds the door open for me, and I take off my hat and scarf that I was wearing to disguise myself before looking around.

"Welcome to our dorm," Changmin says. "Sorry that it's messy."

It's a bit cluttered, but I guess that's to be expected of six men living together in a small space.

I'm self-conscious as Jaesung and Simon, who are sitting on the couches in front of the TV, wave and say hello to me before going back to the video shooter game they're playing.

Apparently no one is surprised I'm here.

"Do you usually throw birthday parties for each other?" I ask Changmin.

"We do, but Byunho is the hardest to please. Which is why we thought we would not do it on camera, and that you should be here."

My cheeks warm. It seems like Changmin has easily accepted the idea that I'm dating his bandmate, though I'm not sure exactly how he was so sure I was—unless he asked Byunho himself.

Haru is in the kitchen smoothing white frosting on a homemade cake with the side of a knife. He beams at me. "Would you like to add strawberries on top?" he asks me.

"Sure!" I agree. I arrange the strawberries in a circle on top of the cake surrounding Byunho's name in Korean.

"It's mocha—a chocolate and coffee cake," Haru tells me with a wink.

"Coffee," I laugh. "Byunho might like it, then."

Now that it's finished, Haru snaps a photo of it with his phone.

Changmin walks into the kitchen to tell us, "Tai and Byunho are getting back from the gym now."

Haru carefully carries the plate holding the cake out into the living room.

The front door opens.

BYUNHO

The guys are acting fucking weird, and I know it's because they've got something planned for my birthday today. I'm not in the mood.

Tai and I go to the gym in the afternoon, and when we come back, the members are gathered in the living room, with Haru holding a cake he must have baked. Hajun is also there.

But the real shock is that Sky is there, too, standing beside the band and smiling.

"Surprise!" everyone cheers.

I've never been good at being the center of positive attention. Even as an idol, it makes me somewhat uncomfortable. And the guys know I hate surprises. But as they start singing, Sky comes to stand beside me. Despite my surprise and worry over the risk of her being here, I'm too glad to see her to be really mad at anyone.

Haru presents the cake, its candles already lit. It's small and round, with white frosting and strawberries on top. The guys finish singing the happy birthday song, and I lean down to blow out the candles.

In that moment, I feel grateful for the family that I've found in this band. Even when the maknae line calls me old.

* * *

AFTER EATING DINNER AND CAKE, we open presents—various pieces of musical equipment and clothing items from my members, until Sky hands me her present in a small bag. She watches me anxiously as I open it and pull out a simple metallic chain bracelet, with a single star charm. It matches with the necklace she made me.

"Thank you," I tell her, my throat tight with emotion. I put the bracelet on, securing it with a clasp around my wrist.

A few minutes later, I make an excuse to show Sky the bedroom I share with Tai, so that we can have a moment alone. Music plays loudly out in the living room as the members continue without us.

"My studio is more personal for me," I say, shutting the door behind us. "This is just where I sleep."

Sky looks around for a moment, taking in the space with two

full beds, two dressers, and the closet space that Tai and I share. She turns to me. "Are you mad that I came here? I really wanted to see you on your birthday."

I sigh and pull her close. "No, I'm not mad. I'm glad I got to see you today. But I'm worried about you. If anything happened to you, I don't know what I would do."

Sky wraps her arms around my waist, fitting her head into the curve of my shoulder. "Nothing's going to happen to me," she promises. Worry comes into her voice. "Was it so obvious that there was something going on between us?" At Seoul Fashion Week, she means. "Do you think Iseul knows?"

"I don't care what Iseul thinks," I say. "You shouldn't, either."

We stay like that for another long moment, holding onto each other. "Don't you want to go hang out with everyone?" she whispers, looking up at me.

"All I want for my birthday is to be alone with you," I murmur, tipping her chin up to kiss her lips. She sighs against my mouth, pressing her body closer. I move backwards slowly, pulling Sky with me down onto my bed so that she's lying on top of me.

"Someone could come in," she says, her face inches from mine.

"They know better," I murmur, looking up at her with hooded eyes before kissing her again.

SKY

Even with all of our clothes on, I melt beneath Byunho's touch as his hands slide across my body. He presses his lips to my throat. "It's been so hard not to be able to see you," he says, voice rough.

Unable to even respond in words, I climb off of him and

move down so that I'm kneeling between his knees on his bed. Laying on his back, he gazes up at me with one brow arched. "What are you doing, babe?"

My cheeks heat. As he watches me, I unlace the tie on his sweatpants.

BYUNHO

I groan as Sky takes my cock in her hands. It grows harder, throbbing beneath her touch, and my heart thunders in my chest. "You don't have to do anything for me," I manage to say. Even as badly as I want it, I feel uncomfortable with receiving something from her without giving anything in return.

"I want to," she says, her voice breathy. She adjusts her position, pushing my knees aside so she can more comfortably lay between them. I twitch as she grips my dick tighter, her cool breath sighing across my hot flesh.

Biting her lip, she looks up at me, holding my gaze, before lowering her head to take my cock in her mouth. Her lips close over the head, her wet tongue almost tentatively swirling across it. I groan again, glad that my bandmates are playing music so loudly. I grip my comforter on my bed beneath me, struggling to keep my hands to myself.

She takes me deeper, moving her head over me in a steady rhythm as one of her hands strokes the shaft. It feels so good that I can't even think, and I feel my self-control slipping away beneath her touch, as it always seems to do. The way she looks with her mouth around my cock is the hottest thing I've ever seen.

"Fuck. Sky. I'm going to come," I growl with the last shred of thought in my brain, but she only bobs her head faster.

I explode into her mouth with a groan. She swallows it all, her tongue massaging the almost painfully sensitive head as she does. My body jerks, every muscle trembling. I stare at her with heavy-lidded eyes as she sits up, breathing just as hard as I am.

"Happy birthday," she says when she finally gets her breath back.

I shake my head at her. "Come here," I say in a voice she can't argue with. She crawls on top of me, laying on my chest. "You've already given me so much more than I deserve, Sky. You are the only present I want."

We lay like that for a while, lingering in this moment of safety, ignoring the uncertainty and fear that exists in the world outside of this room.

TWENTY-SIX

66 Love so good, feels like a thriller / It's begun / This
is an emergency"

— "Love 119," RIIZE

SKY

THE NEXT AFTERNOON, I decide to stay late at work.
We're finishing up the stage outfits for KOSMIC's world tour,
which starts with a show at a stadium in Seoul in just a few
days. If I look around after hours, I might just find another clue.

It's a desperate idea, but staying at the department after
hours is a perfect opportunity to search my colleagues' work
stations, something I can't do during the day.

Hanging out in a bathroom stall for fifteen minutes after
everyone else leaves, I text Byunho to tell him what I'm doing.
He must be busy, because he doesn't respond.

I take a deep breath and leave the bathroom.

The lights are off in the large, cavernous room where the
styling department does our work, only a little bit of natural

light filtering through the windows up high near the tall ceiling. The mannequins clothed with in-progress designs become dark figures lurking in the shadows. I consider turning the overhead lights back on, but the lights could be seen and anyone coming to turn them off could find me and start asking questions about why I'm still here.

I cross the room, my footsteps echoing off the concrete walls. Reaching Eunjung's workstation, I use my phone flashlight to look around. A photo of her husband and son sits on the desk. I examine a notepad with her handwriting. It doesn't match the spidery writing on the note I received. I move on.

Ms. Goh's desk is next.

It doesn't have many personal touches. Although not disorganized, her desk is covered in inventory lists and scattered supplies. I move a stack of files. I pause when beneath it, I see the same notepaper the note was written on. An off-white square with dark blue lines.

Her handwriting doesn't match, though.

A loud clatter behind me shatters the silence of the room.

I spin around, pointing my phone flashlight in the direction of the sound. My heart pounds unevenly.

"Hello? Who's there?" I ask in Korean, my voice shaky.

Shit, that's what someone in a horror movie says right before they get murdered. I squint into the darkness. There are footsteps, moving quickly away from me.

I creep cautiously over to where I heard the original sound.

It came from my work station.

One of Byunho's stage outfits that I was working on today has been shredded into ribbons.

My blood turns to ice.

Then, off to my left, what I thought was a mannequin moves.

A scream tears out of my throat.

A person steps into a rectangle of pale light from the high windows.

Her face is familiar.

"Miyoung?" I gasp.

It's Stylist Goh's daughter.

BYUNHO

I'm staying late at work to check something

Sky texted me, twenty minutes ago. It's almost 6 PM, and the members and I have just wrapped up a nine-hour practice for our upcoming concert.

As I stare at my phone, my heart begins to pound for a completely different reason than dance practice. "Fuck," I mutter under my breath. My hair sticks to the back of my neck with sweat.

"What is it?" Changmin asks me.

It could be nothing, but it also could mean that Sky is in danger.

"I need to go," I say, grabbing my sweatshirt and bag. I jog out of the practice room, trying to figure out which way is the shortest to get to the styling department.

As I run, I dial Aera's phone number.

SKY

Miyoung just stares at me, her expression somehow sad.

"Are you the one who did this?" I ask, gesturing to the ruined costume.

Her gaze is accusatory. "I told you to stay away from him," she says.

My heart jumps. "Why would you do this?"

Miyoung has something in her hands. A pair of metal scissors gleams in the darkness. She turns them over in her hands, seeming suddenly lost in thought. "I just wanted to make my eomma proud of me at first, so I went to fashion school. Then my eomma got the job here working with Byunho-oppa. I was so happy." Her voice sounds high and breathy, like a little girl's, even though she's only a few years younger than I am.

"But I couldn't get the job here... I couldn't work here with Byunho-oppa." A piercing, angry gaze meets mine. "He loves you, not me. But you went to their dorm on his birthday. I saw you."

My pulse thumps with adrenaline. I take a slow step backward, not wanting to provoke her with any sudden movement.

I have to go around her to get to the door.

I run.

My phone flashlight bounces around crazily as I sprint into the tall racks of clothing storage. I hear the echo of footsteps behind me.

I turn several tight corners, then stop to listen. I can hear my heartbeat and ragged breathing, but nothing else. I can see the pathway to the door, but Miyoung could be hiding anywhere between here and there, ready to jump out at me.

The overhead lights flicker on.

"Sky!" Byunho's voice yells.

I gasp. "Watch out!" is all I can yell back. In response, I hear a clatter of footsteps up ahead. I charge after the sound.

Miyoung shrieks as she runs toward Byunho, holding the scissors in one of her hands. He stands near the entrance, horror written in his expression.

BYUNHO

"Watch out!" Sky screams, her voice cracking with fear.

A girl runs toward me, screaming, a pair of scissors held in her hands.

Sky jumps on the girl's back, almost knocking the girl down. The girl tries to shake her off, but Sky hugs her from behind, grabbing her wrists to try to take control of the weapon.

I lunge forward to help, terror gripping my heart at seeing Sky in danger. The unknown girl is sobbing as she screams, incomprehensible sentences pouring out of her. I manage to pry the scissors out of the girl's hands, taking them away.

Behind us, the door opens, and security guards stream through the door, surrounding us with noise and chaos.

Aera must have called them.

As the girl is hauled away, Sky and I look at each other.

Sky's face is pale, tears streaming down her face.

Something inside of me breaks.

* * *

"IT'S a good thing that you called me when you did," Aera says to me after I've finished giving my statement at the police station. Sky is giving her statement now. There was a professional interpreter with her, but neither of us are allowed to be in the room with her. Our statements have to be given separately to ensure an accurate record.

So Aera and I wait outside the interrogation room, seated on uncomfortable chairs, unlikely allies in this mess.

I hate it, but there's nothing I can do. Sky insisted she was fine, though I know that can't be true. Not after what she's just gone through.

After receiving my phone call, Aera had gone to the security department and checked the security cameras. Seeing that something was wrong, she sent CKM's security team while the police were on their way.

The girl called Miyoung was a saesang, a stalker fan. Her mother, Head Stylist Goh, a member of CKM's styling department, had started working at CKM a couple of years ago, and since then Miyoung had used that connection to stalk the members of KOSMIC, particularly me.

Stylist Goh had no idea.

When Miyoung, attending work with her mother, noticed the tension between me and Sky, she became suspicious and began stalking Sky until she discovered that we were dating. After that, she began sabotaging Sky's costumes for me in an attempt to get Sky fired, and when that didn't work, she left Sky the threatening note during Seoul Fashion Week.

Sky had been alone in the dark with that saesang. If I hadn't seen her text, if I hadn't gotten there in time…

Aera's clear voice interrupts my spiraling thoughts. "It's not your fault," she says.

I turn to stare at the chaebol heiress sitting beside me. "What?"

"It's not your fault that this happened," she repeats. "I can see you thinking that, but it's not."

My brow creases. "How do you know what I'm thinking?"

"Because that's what I thought, when the scandal about me and Hajun broke. That it was my fault, for being who I am." Aera sighs, staring across the room at the clock on the wall, which ticks slowly towards midnight. "Your relationship with Sky wasn't a mistake that led to this event happening. This happened because this world creates sick people who can't comprehend or tolerate others' happiness."

Before I can respond, the door opens and an officer escorts

Sky out of the interrogation room. Sky looks tired and pale, and the sight of her feels like a needle stabbed through my heart.

"You're all free to go," the officer says.

"Thank you for all of your help," Aera replies, taking Sky's hand. We head out of the police station and into the night.

Sky says nothing, and it takes all of my self control not to take her into my arms, check for anything that the paramedics might have missed, and never let her go.

The company driver is idling on the curb.

"I want to go home," Sky finally says, her voice small.

Aera nods. "Okay, we'll go home. I can stay with you tonight if you want."

"I mean... I want to go back to the U.S."

At those words, the world beneath my feet seems to stop spinning.

SKY

I don't meet Byunho's eyes as I announce that I want to go home to the U.S.

For the past few hours, all I can see when I look at him is how close he came to being hurt. My stomach is tied into knots.

"I want to see my family. I just... need some time," I explain, trying to hold it together, not to cry. If I cry, then Byunho will try to comfort me, and if I let him do that, I won't be able to make myself leave.

Thankfully, neither he nor Aera tries to talk me out of it. We get in the company car. Byunho is dropped off at the idol dorm, his eyes holding mine for a long moment before the car pulls away from the curb.

Only when I can no longer see him do I finally let myself cry. Aera holds tightly onto my hand.

The next day, the paperwork is filed approving a break from my position at CKM.

"I don't... I don't know when I'll be able to come back," I tell Aera.

"You can return to this job whenever you're ready," she promises me. "Just focus on time with your family and whatever you need to feel better, okay?"

I take the next flight out of Incheon International Airport, leaving behind South Korea and the love of my life.

TWENTY-SEVEN

" Me without you, I'm fake / Sky without light, black / Everyday is meaningless"

— "You Calling My Name," GOT7

BYUNHO

HAJUN STOPPED by our dorm not long after the incident.

I was sitting on the edge of my bed in my room, staring at the wall, numbness spreading throughout my body. I hadn't had time to process what had happened. The girl running toward me with the scissors, Sky risking injury to restrain her, the police... Sky announcing she was going to go back to the U.S....

"What are you doing here?" Tai asked someone outside our door, his voice surprised.

"I'm here to speak with Byunho," said Hajun's voice. A moment later, he pushed open the cracked door to mine and Tai's room.

"Hey," Hajun said, coming into the room. He stopped a few

feet away, and I could feel his gaze on me, but I didn't look at him.

"What do you want?" I asked, much more harshly than Tai had.

Hajun didn't snap back at me like I expected, like he always used to do. He allowed a moment of silence to pass before responding. "Aera told me what happened. I decided to stop by."

"Aren't you busy?" The question didn't come out with the bite I intended it to have.

Hajun sighed. "It's going to be alright, hyung. You just need to give her time."

When I didn't respond, Hajun took the hint and left me alone. But he must have told the others everything that had happened, because everyone has been treating me like I'm a bomb ready to explode.

The first concert of our world tour is tonight in Seoul, to a sold-out stadium. It's the largest concert we've performed so far in our career.

I put all of my energy into the performance, going through the motions that are ingrained in my muscle memory from thousands of hours of practice. But when the concert is over, I have nothing left but an empty pit in my stomach.

"Great job, guys," Changmin says as we head backstage after our last song. The cheers of the crowd echo in our ears, loud enough that even with our in-ear pieces, it was deafening. Jaesung is grinning ear-to-ear, and Simon laughs at something Tai says. Everyone is in a celebratory mood, except for me. I need to get out of here.

I notice the concerned glance Haru gives me as I stride straight toward the dressing rooms.

After changing out of my stage clothes, I leave the venue and drive to the studio. I need to take advantage of having access to all of my recording equipment before we go to Japan and I'll be forced to work on my laptop and with only the few smaller pieces of equipment I can bring with me.

After shows in Tokyo and Osaka, we're coming back to Korea for performances at several different award shows, then touring Southeast Asia with dates in Manila, Singapore, Macau, Hong Kong, Jakarta, Taipei, and Bangkok. Then we'll fly to South America, Europe, and the U.S.

I won't have time to breathe during the next five months. Now is the only time I have to be truly alone and work on my music, and there is something inside of me that compels me to keep working no matter how physically exhausted I am. Something like desperation. I haven't been able to sleep, anyway.

My second mixtape, which I began just after returning with Sky from Busan, is almost complete. One of the company producers always said that my lyric writing style didn't suit love songs. Hajun, Changmin, and Tai were better at writing those types of songs. I usually write to the darker themes on our albums.

And yet, the songs on my new mixtape are different. They're all about Sky. They're all about how she makes me feel.

I didn't think I could love someone the way that I love her.

Sky hasn't texted me since she got back to the U.S., and I don't know what to say. It's possible she blames me for the danger our relationship put her in. That would be fair.

It's ironic that the only thing I ever wanted, to have a career in music, means nothing to me now compared to the happiness of being with her.

I write it down.

TWENTY-EIGHT

> This cold season is so long / There is not a single
> flower / I'm still the same from that day"
>
> — "HANN (Alone in winter)," (G)I-DLE

SKY

THE LAWN of my childhood home is buried in snow. I look
outside my second-story bedroom window at the street, which
the late-season snowstorm last night blanketed in white. It's
March, and I've been staying at my parents' house for about five
months. My twenty-fifth birthday is in a week, but I have no
idea who I am or what I'm doing with my life anymore.

I thought it would be a short break, that I would go home,
take some time and space to think for a month or so about what
to do... about my position at CKM Entertainment, and about my
relationship with Byunho. But I haven't come any closer to an
answer.

For the first few months, I was having nightmares about
what happened. About running through the dark, being chased

through the maze of clothing racks. I didn't reach them in time. In the end, just before I wake up, Byunho gets stabbed in the chest. There's so much blood, so dark and red. I've never seen anything like that in real life, outside of movies, but I see it so clearly in my dreams.

"I just feel like I didn't go through anything that bad," I told my younger brother after one nightmare, sitting on the edge of his bed. Even though he had to go to school in the morning, he didn't mind me waking him up to talk in the middle of the night. "No one died. No one even got hurt. Why can't I get over it?" I was filled with rage at myself.

Tony shook his head. "It's not about what happened, it's about what it felt like."

I don't know how he knew exactly what to say to make me feel better. I laughed a little at my younger brother's serious face. "You're a teenage boy, how are you so wise?"

He rolled his eyes at me.

I've been taking medication to help with the nightmares, which have stopped happening so regularly these last two months. I can sleep through the night. I feel more like myself again.

Aera texts me every day. Most of the time, we don't talk about anything important. But she did tell me that KOSMIC is having a concert in Newark, one of the last stops of their world tour. She said that if I wanted to go, she would send me a backstage pass.

I could see Byunho again.

Although after I left him for almost half a year while he's been on his world tour, he might have moved on. He might have decided I'm not worth waiting for. The problem was, I had no idea if he wanted to see me, and I was too scared to contact him.

Then, while I'm sitting by my window reading a book one afternoon, three days before the concert, Changmin calls me out of the blue. I pick up, feeling almost panicked. What if something happened to Byunho?

"Hello, Sky," says his familiar voice.

"Changmin? Is everything okay?"

"Everything's okay," he quickly reassures me. "How are you?"

I relax a little, but there must be some other reason he called me. "I'm fine. How's the tour?"

"It's good. Tonight is our Chicago concert. Sky..." He pauses, his voice softening. "I'm not calling to blame you. I know what happened wasn't your fault. It wasn't. I'm calling to ask you to meet with Byunho."

For a moment, I get deja vu for when Changmin called me to ask me to come to the dorm for Byunho's birthday. Except now, things are so different.

"After what happened, I know you needed time..." Changmin pauses, switching to Korean, choosing his words slowly and carefully so that I understand exactly what he's trying to say. "But I'm asking you to speak with him, because he won't ask you himself. I've never seen him like this. The last time I saw him this way was when we were trainees..."

My heart aches. I feel tears prick my eyes, and I squeeze them shut.

"It's up to you to decide whether you want to be with him. But I think you owe it to him to tell him what you decide in person, so he can stop waiting for you."

With a stomach-dropping sensation, I realize he's right. I owe it to Byunho and myself to have this conversation. Whatever the outcome.

"Okay," I say. "I'll be there."

TWENTY-NINE

> I'll sing along to you the same melody / I cry and
> laugh along with you / This night where I give all
> my love"

— "Headliner," SEVENTEEN

BYUNHO

ANOTHER CITY, another concert.

The western leg of our world tour has drained me more than I thought was possible. From Latin America, where we played concerts in São Paulo, Santiago, and Mexico City, to Europe, where we performed in Copenhagen, Amsterdam, Berlin, London, Paris, and Madrid, I've been unable to find the previous enjoyment that I felt in performing.

I've started to hate my fame, even resent my fans who look up at me on the stage with such adoration. What is the purpose of all of this? I don't know anymore.

But it's gotten worse since coming to the U.S. Atlanta, Orlando, Austin, Los Angeles, San Francisco, Chicago...

I keep waiting, hoping that Sky will be there. But she isn't.

Now we're in Newark, New Jersey, at the venue preparing to go onstage. It's our last concert before returning to Korea.

Sitting in the dressing area, leaning my head back against the wall, I listen to music with my eyes closed. I hear the faint sound of someone's footsteps, feel the presence of someone standing close to me. I assume it's one of my bandmates, until I smell it.

The sweet floral scent of her perfume.

My eyes fly open. And she's there, in front of me.

Her warm brown eyes watch me with uncertainty, her hands twisted in front of her, her bottom lip caught between her teeth. She's even more breathtaking than I remembered.

"Sky," I breathe, unable to believe it.

SKY

It isn't as easy as you'd think to get into the concert venue. Despite my VIP backstage pass that Aera sent me, security is tight and they are suspicious enough to call the band's manager to check that I'm supposed to be here.

Sangjin comes out to get me with, to his credit, only a little irritation.

"I'm not going to ask why you're here, but please don't say anything to upset Byunho before the concert," he says. "That's the last thing I need. If you're going to break his heart, wait until after he's done performing."

I'm too overwhelmed to take his comment personally.

"Also, sign this." He hands me a tablet with an NDA document on it. I look at him in disbelief, wondering if he's joking. He isn't. I take the stylus and sign the bottom line.

Sangjin leads me through a maze of hallways to the artist dressing room.

Jaesung sees me first and let out a small shriek of joy before jumping up off the couch he's sitting on and dashing toward me. "Noona!" Skirting to a halt in front of me, he hesitates with his arms out for just a moment, as if not sure it's appropriate to hug me.

I throw my arms around him. He picks me up and spins me around, making me laugh.

By now, Changmin has also seen me and crossed the room to stand in front of me.

"Thank you for coming," Changmin says. His eyes are warm as he smiles at me. "It's good to see you well."

"Thanks," I say, smiling back at him. But my smile fades quickly as I wonder if Byunho even wants to see me.

As if reading the distraction on my face, Changmin gestures behind him. "He's over there. Don't worry... he'll be glad to see you."

I nod. I guess it's time. Taking a deep breath, I cross the room. My rising anxiety makes my stomach lurch.

Around the corner, Byunho is slumped on a low couch against the wall, his eyes closed. His hair is back to its natural black, and he's wearing his stage outfit, a tight fitted black jacket and pants lined with sequins that catch the light and shimmer darkly. For a moment, I think he's sleeping, but as I step closer, his eyes fly open.

"Sky." My name is rough in his throat. Slowly, he takes his earbuds out of his ears, staring at me with his dark brows furrowed as if he can't believe I'm standing there in front of me. Around his neck is the necklace that I made for him.

My heart contracts painfully. "I thought I'd come see you perform," I say softly, although the words are entirely insufficient for the emotions creating a storm inside of me—fear, happiness, regret, and hope.

The slightest smile touches Byunho's lips, although his eyes remain locked on mine. "I wouldn't want to disappoint my number one fan."

I can't help but smile at his half-hearted attempt at a joke. I start to say something more, I don't know what—but Haru appears out of nowhere.

"Noona!" he exclaims, just like Jaesung had earlier, a wide smile spreading across his face upon seeing me. "Are you going to watch our show? It's starting soon." He turns to his bandmate. "Hyung, we have to go now."

Byunho nods and stands up, which means he's suddenly standing very close to me. He holds my gaze. "We'll talk after the show," he says, his tone holding a promise that even if I wanted to, I couldn't disagree with.

My breath stolen by his proximity, I can only nod in agreement. He goes around me and follows Haru to the rest of the group, looking back once to ensure I'm still behind them.

I quickly fall behind KOSMIC and their entourage of staff. I recognize a few other employees. I nod politely at them and they nod politely back, though I think I catch a few odd looks.

Oh, well.

I'm standing without a clue where to go or what to do when Sangjin appears, seemingly out of nowhere. "Come with me," he says.

I blink at him in shock, but obey his command. He brings me through some narrow hallways and several flights of stairs to a private box with a clear view of the stage and the big screens. "Thank you," I say. He flaps a hand as if to say "whatever" and sits in the back of the box, pulling out his phone.

I go up to the balcony and look out at the vast crowd, thousands of lightsticks waving in the dark.

Fog surrounds the empty stage, lit up by flashing red and yellow lights. Bass notes pulse through the ground, resonating in my bones. The stage suddenly goes dark, and the crowd roars in excitement.

Low lights come back on to show the six silhouettes of the KOSMIC members, enveloped in fog. As the opening beats of their latest title song explode, the spotlights come on and the screens show the beginning of the choreography.

I stand for the whole show near the balcony, watching the performance. I've never seen KOSMIC perform a full, two-and-a-half-hour long show before. The energy is infectious, the way the band feeds off of the crowd's energy and the fans' excitement mounts even higher as the show goes on.

But even with everything else happening, I can't take my eyes off of Byunho. His confidence, his intensity, his passion... all of it is magnified on stage, and every time his dark eyes stare into the camera, it's like he's looking at me. My heart pounds, and I have to lean on the railing for support. I can't look away.

Before the encore, the show pauses for the members to say their thank-yous to the crowd. Each member takes a turn saying something.

"New Jersey... It's been a long journey to be here together," Changmin says, looking out at the crowd. "We're very thankful to you... for standing by us even when there are hardships, or even though you've had to wait for us for a long time. We know how much you have done for us. We don't know yet everything that the future will hold, but we promise to keep working hard for you. Thank you."

When Changmin finishes his speech, Byunho lifts his mic to his lips and waits patiently for the cheers to quiet before speaking. "Tonight is the last night of our world tour. To be honest..." He looks into the camera, and I realize, heart pounding, that he's speaking to me.

His dark eyes shine with unshed tears, and the crowd hushes to listen to him. "I have been carrying a heavy burden inside of me because of things that happened in the past. I know it's not easy or peaceful to love me." He pauses to swallow, blinking rapidly so that his tears won't fall. "But I hope you will give us another chance."

The crowd cries and cheers, but I know that his words are for me.

THIRTY

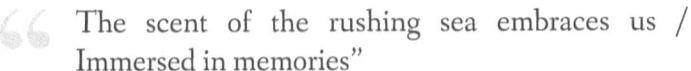 The scent of the rushing sea embraces us /
Immersed in memories"

— "Sunset Sky," ASTRO

BYUNHO

WE PERFORM one last song before saying our goodbyes,
bowing, and walking off stage. In the rush of staff and venue
employees, I search for Sky's face.

But I don't see her anywhere.

My heart pounds with fear. What if she left after hearing
my speech? What if she's decided she doesn't want to give me
another chance?

On our way to the vans that will transport us to our hotel for
the night, I spot Manager Sangjin speaking with a member of
our security team. I stop him by catching his arm. "Where is
she?"

He sighs, not appreciative of being growled at. "I sent her to your hotel, so you may speak in private." He emphasizes the last two words.

"I wasn't aware that sending women to our hotel room was a service you offered, Sangjin-nim," Simon quips.

"It's not," Sangjin grumbles.

But I'm no longer paying attention to their conversation, focused on getting to the hotel as fast as possible.

SKY

At the end of the concert, Sangjin summons his assistant, a man only a few years older than myself, and instructs me to go with him to KOSMIC's hotel. When I try to protest, saying that I can wait for Byunho backstage, Sangjin gives me a look of such disapproval and annoyance that I immediately shut up and do as he says. To think I once thought Byunho was the grumpiest man I'd ever met.

The assistant manager brings me to KOSMIC's reserved hotel floor and shows me into a suite with several adjoining bedrooms which I assume belong to three of the members, including Byunho.

I take a seat on one of the couches in the center of the room, and Sangjin's assistant leaves me alone, no questions asked and barely a handful of words exchanged.

Anxiety builds as I wait.

It's a relief that after everything, he wants to give our relationship another chance. But I can't just throw myself into his arms and live happily ever after, can I? It's more complicated than that. Aera and Hajun's story taught me that much.

I pace over to the curtained windows along one wall and look out, watching cars go past and multicolored neon lights shine. I glance up at the sky. You can never see the stars in the city.

The suite door opens, and it's just Byunho, now changed out of his stage clothes.

He comes into the room, letting the door shut behind him. Both of us gravitate to the sitting area in the center of the room, him taking a seat on the couch, me on an armchair. Neither of us knows exactly how to start.

"Where is everyone?" I ask.

Byunho clears his throat. "They went to the other suite to give us privacy."

I nod. "The concert was incredible," I say, a laugh slipping out. "I wasn't disappointed."

He chuckles, a slight smile curving up the corner of his mouth. "Thanks."

But the levity is fleeting.

"There's something I need to say..." I can't hold his dark, intense gaze as I search for words. "I'm sorry for leaving you after what happened. I didn't think..." My eyes tear up. "I didn't think I should be around after our relationship caused you to be attacked. And I was so scared. It's taken all this time for me to feel safe again, and I didn't know if I ever would."

Byunho's gaze softens, and I see his fists clench at his sides. "Sky," he says. "It's not your fault. You fought for me. You *saved* me. You have nothing to apologize for. Leaving Korea... It was difficult for me, but I understand it. You never asked to be put in that situation." He pauses, brow furrowed.

"And I... what I said at the concert may have put too much pressure on you. I'm sorry for that." He takes a deep breath before meeting my eyes. "But while you were gone, I finished a mixtape. Working on it gave me clarity. I realized... that I love you."

The tears in my eyes start to fall. "Byunho, I... I love you too." The words release a heaviness inside my chest that I hadn't known was there.

He comes and kneels in front of me, his hands rising to cup my face. The pads of his thumbs swipe away my tears.

"What do we do now?" I ask. His eyes hold mine with a reverence I can't believe is for me.

"Whatever you want," he says softly. "If you want to come out as a couple, we can have the company make a statement."

My heart skips a beat. "No."

"We can keep our relationship a secret for now, then," he says.

I nod. "That's what I want, for both our sakes. Also, with the tour over, if you're free... there's somewhere I want to go with you."

BYUNHO

During the drive to Massachusetts, I play my unreleased mixtape for Sky, and we talk. I tell her about all of the places we went on tour and everything we did, and she tells me about her family and the seaside town where she grew up.

"My parents don't know you're coming," Sky tells me. "But don't worry, they'll love you."

Her reassurance does nothing to ease my apprehension. Though I want to meet her family, I'm not sure they'll believe I'm the best person for her, given that our relationship caused something traumatic to happen to her. More than just that, I'm a foreigner and they're American. But I'm willing to try to prove to them that I can make her happy.

We pull into the driveway of a large brick house and park in front of a garage. There's a tree in the yard, branches sprouting with green spring leaves and flowers.

"We're home!" Sky says. She smiles at me and takes my hand. "Come on, let's go meet my family."

SKY

My parents are more than a little shocked to see a K-Pop idol in their living room, but they recover quickly. It's a Sunday afternoon, so Papa was reading a book and Mom was doing yard work when we walked through the front door.

After the initial shock has passed, Mom brings chips and dip and Papa offers Byunho a beer, while my brother awkwardly perches on the couch next to our equally awkward father.

Seeing Byunho in my childhood living room is surreal. He sits on the shorter couch, and I sit beside him.

"I watched all your music videos when I learned my daughter was going to work with you," my mom tells Byunho, as a way to start conversation.

He smiles. Only I can see how tense he is, from the set of his shoulders. "Thank you, Ms. Flores."

My mom begins to pepper him with questions, about his work, his family, what working with me is like. Byunho takes it all with the same patience he would give to an interview at an American talkshow. His English has improved so much over the course of our relationship that I only have to step in to clarify a few things.

"Okay, Mom, that's enough interrogation. We're going to take a walk, but we'll be back for dinner." I take Byunho's hand as we go back outside. He pulls a face mask out of his pocket and puts it on, even though we're in a quiet suburban neighborhood.

"Sorry for all of that," I say. "Thank you for meeting them."

"I hope I did everything right." Byunho's brow furrows.

I laugh, finding his uncertainty endearing. "You were perfect. I know it's hard to do, but try to relax. You're safe with me and my family. I promise."

He grips my hand tighter in response.

We keep walking, all the way to the beach. It's cold enough out that there's hardly anyone else on the beach, save an older couple and their dog. Byunho pulls his mask down and breathes in the salty air.

The sun is setting behind us, painting the whole sky in soft oranges, pinks, and purples. Sea gulls caw overhead and hop across the sand, and the grass on the dune behind us blows gently in the wind. Stars begin to appear in the deep purple and blue above the ocean.

The pain and fear that I have been carrying for months now is eased. Not gone, but bearable. I know what I want, and what I want is the man beside me.

Not a single part of my dream turned out how I expected. But now, I see that it's better than anything I could have imagined, because I found him.

"I've decided I want to come back to Korea and continue working at CKM. I liked my job, and I'm not going to let what happened get in the way of my dream," I tell Byunho, smiling a little as I add, "And because it's where you are."

He looks at me with a softness that fills my heart. "Then there's something you should know," he says.

"What is it?" I ask.

"I'm going to the military soon," he says. "Next year. Changmin and I might get our deadline extended, but it's not confirmed yet, and I wanted you to know that there's a chance I might have to leave soon."

I hadn't realized his mandatory military enlistment would happen so soon for him. He turned 26 only just before I left. The group has only been active for five years, but next year Byunho and Changmin will both turn 28, the deadline for mandatory service.

"I'll be serving for almost two years. I know it's a long time to wait, but... you are the light of my life, Sky. When I do come back, I want to be with you. So I'm asking you if you could wait that long for me." His dark eyes shine as the breeze blows his reddish-brown hair against his cheek.

Tears fill my eyes. I step forward into Byunho's chest, inhaling his scent of coffee and sandalwood. He wraps his arms around me, holding me close, and I feel his lips against my forehead. "I don't want to be away from you for that long," I say. "I feel like I've already wasted so much time. But you've already waited for me. I will wait for you."

I feel Byunho's fingers beneath my chin, tipping my head up. He leans down, covering my mouth with his own. The kiss is as gentle and as beautiful as the sunset.

BECOME A MEMBER OF KOSMIC'S
OFFICIAL FANCLUB, INFINITY

Subscribe to the Kosmic official website for exclusive bonus content like sneak peeks of upcoming KOSMIC series books, bonus stories, playlists, and more:

erinkayauthor.com

And don't forget to subscribe to author Erin Kay's social media:

Instagram @erinkay_author
TikTok @erin_k_books
Twitter @erin_kay_books

KOSMIC FOREVER

THE KOSMIC HEART EPILOGUE

Turn the page to read *Kosmic Forever*, the epilogue to Book 1, *Kosmic Heart*.

A year after their dating scandal, Aera and Hajun must choose between a life of secrecy or a life together beneath the spotlight.

Kosmic Forever takes place months after the events of KOSMIC Book 1 and partially during the events of Book 2, *Kosmic Kiss*.

This exclusive epilogue can be found only in the physical edition of *Kosmic Kiss* and on the author's website.

A BRIEF HISTORY: THE CHAEBOL
FAMILY BEHIND CKM ENT.

CKM Entertainment is a subsidiary company of CKM Group, a management and production agency for actors and musicians. CKM Ent. was founded in 1999 and has produced and managed various successful actors and musicians, including K-Pop groups. The two most successful and currently active K-Pop groups with the company are the boy group KOSMIC and the girl group BADKITTY.

CKM Group, owned by Kim Chulwoo, is a conglomerate of companies in various sectors and was founded by Kim Chulwoo's grandfather, Kim Changkyun (CKM). CKM Group is run by a board of directors which includes Kim Chulwoo as its Chairman. On this board of directors are the other CEOs, COOs, and CFOs Chulwoo has appointed to each of the Group's subsidiary companies. The current Vice Chairwoman of CKM Group is Kim Chulwoo's daughter, Kim Aera, an alum of Harvard and Chulwoo's only child. In addition to the role of Vice Chairwoman, she also holds the position of COO (Chief Operations Officer) of CKM Entertainment.

Some notable companies within CKM Group include an airline, founded by Chulwoo's father, engineering firms, sustainable energy companies, agricultural management companies, various food processing facilities and food distribution services, a pharmaceutical company, a waste management company, and other transportation companies. Of all of these companies owned by CKM Group, CKM

Entertainment is an outlier in that it provides entertainment rather than essential services.

When Kim Chulwoo inherited CKM Group from his father, Kim Changwook, he instituted new management processes. One of CKM Group's key tenants now is its emphasis on sustainability, which it applies to all of the above industries. For example, Group's airline prioritizes use of biofuel for jet fuel, which some of its agricultural and food processing companies play a role in manufacturing. Most of the airline's flights are powered by jet biofuel and only fly full flights, helping to reduce carbon emissions. CKM Group also invests a significant amount of money into climate research and the conservation of nature and wildlife habitat in South Korea.

While not strictly the most profitable approach to running a large corporation, Chulwoo has stated about the changes he's made to the corporation, "CKM Group is committed to progress, not profit." This statement showcases its CEO's character, further demonstrated by the private, reserved figure's unconventional personal history.

Kim Chulwoo's wife, famous ballad singer and actress Kang Areum, founded CKM Entertainment in 1999. The entertainment agency was a gift from Chulwoo to his wife after their marriage in 1997. Their marriage was a shocking scandal of the late 90s—Chulwoo was engaged to the daughter of another chaebol family, but called off the engagement and married a well-known entertainer instead. As Kim Chulwoo was the only heir to CKM Group, this made it an even bigger scandal and the family lost some face in the upper class of Korea, their status only maintained by their financial power.

Kang Areum ran CKM Ent. as its CEO until she passed away from cancer. During the years that she ran the company, it grew to become one of the "big four/five" of entertainment agencies in South Korea. Chulwoo took over as its CEO after his wife's passing, rather than entrusting its management to one of his wife's employees.

CKM Ent.'s hit boy group KOSMIC debuted in 2019 and became an international success.

In 2022, current CKM Group Vice Chairwoman, Kim Aera, was revealed to be in a relationship with Yun Hajun, a K-Pop idol from the boy group KOSMIC. A former manager of KOSMIC broke company rules, along with his employment contract, and sold photographs of the couple to the press to pay off a personal debt. The public was shocked by the relationship between a popular K-Pop idol and a chaebol heiress. The scandal was an echo of the scandal of Kim Aera's parents.

At a press conference in response to the scandal, it was announced that CKM Ent. would change its dating policies for its idols, removing the restrictive dating ban. Despite this change, as a result of the scandal Yun Hajun left KOSMIC and began his career as a solo artist under CKM Entertainment.

It is currently unknown to the world whether Kim Aera and Yun Hajun's relationship survived the scandal of being revealed to the public.

"You and me, an unending history
    Oh, you became my universe
    The story of us"

— "The Astronaut," Jin

KOSMIC FOREVER

AERA

I pull into the parking lot of the villa complex in Samseong-dong, the security guard waving me through the gates when I tell him my name and show my ID.

Hajun's car is already parked in one of the roomy spaces beneath the high walls and the neatly manicured hedges. My stomach flips at the sight. I park in one of the empty spaces, and take several deep breaths before I unbuckle my seat belt and climb out.

A familiar figure waits outside the front door of the high-rise villa complex, his hands tucked into the pockets of his brown trench coat as he speaks with a shorter man in a nice suit who must be Maeng Chungee, the real estate agent.

When he notices my approach, Hajun pauses whatever he's saying, a smile curving his lips as he watches me with his steady, warm gaze. My heart trips over itself, but I don't show it.

"You must be Miss Kim." The real estate agent greets me respectfully. Surely Mr. Maeng knows who we are, but he deals with wealthy or celebrity clients every day and has already signed the non-disclosure agreement about this meeting.

"I hope you weren't waiting long," I reply. My eyes catch

Hajun's. His hair is dyed back to its natural black and getting longer, his bangs starting to fall into his eyes, reminding me of how he looked when I met him years ago. Though it's only been a few days since we last saw one another, the ache to brush his hair out of his eyes is nearly unbearable.

"Not at all. Will your parents not be joining you?"

There's an awkward pause.

"My family lives in Jeju, so they can't make it today," Hajun answers smoothly.

"My abeoji is a busy man." And he doesn't know this is happening.

"Ah. I see." I can see Mr. Maeng trying not to frown, as his gaze travels down to my left hand. Looking for an engagement ring.

I fold my hands behind my back, so that he can't see I'm not wearing one.

But he seems appeased enough by our explanations that he asks no more personal questions. At least for now. "Well, shall we go inside?"

Once inside the elegant lobby of the complex, we take the elevator to one of the top floors. After Mr. Maeng types a code into a keypad, the door opens into an entry hallway with dark wood cabinets and shelves on either side. I hang my scarf on a peg in one of the closets. We take off our shoes and slip on the provided slippers before stepping out of the entryway and into the villa.

"Here is the living space."

A spacious living area greets us, with shining wooden floors and large windows looking out onto the pale blue Han River, the skyline and mountains rising beyond. The autumn leaves add bright brush strokes of red, yellow and orange to the canvas of the city. My breath stolen, I sneak a glance at Hajun's reaction, to see if he too is imagining this space as our own. He gives me a small, almost shy smile.

"This space is central to the rest of the villa. So you can go this way, into the entertaining space, or you can go this way, into the private quarters. Shall we look at the entertaining space first?"

The entertaining space, as he calls it, includes a dining room overlooking the river with a crystal chandelier. The spacious kitchen beyond it is modern, with black-lacquered cabinets and marble countertops, a large pantry, and even a room intended for a live-in housekeeper. Growing up, my nanny lived in one of these. Although Hajun and I may need some help keeping a space like this clean, I can't imagine sharing our private space with anyone. After everything we've gone through, our privacy is sacred.

Which is the reason we're doing this—finding a place of our own. It's overdue for me to move out of my father's house, even though we rarely see each other at home. Living there reminds me too much of being a teenager. Even my room hasn't changed.

Passing back through the kitchen and dining area, Mr. Maeng shows us the study and series of other rooms on the other side of the living space.

"And through here is the master suite."

A short hallway leads to a modest-sized bedroom with another window facing the river greets us, adjoined by a large walk-in dress room as well as a giant bathroom, complete with a jacuzzi tub. My mind flashes back to that one night at an expensive love hotel with Hajun, and I try very hard not to blush. Hajun, knowing me too well, smirks at me behind the real estate agent's back.

We head back out into the living room.

"Well, there you have it." Mr. Maeng grins. "I suppose the

wedding must be soon, if you plan to buy and move in together within the next few months."

My chest tightens. Before I have to come up with an excuse, Hajun answers him. "The wedding date is not set yet. I'll be the one making the purchase, with the idea that she will be joining me in the future."

This is a lie. One that feels like a punch to the stomach.

We're not even engaged. I'm sending Hajun half of the money for the villa, so even though the property has to be under his name, we're both paying for it. And we're planning on living together as soon as he gets the keys, although I'll be covering my tracks by renting a separate place in my own name.

Because how else are we to be together without raising another scandal?

However, money must overcome propriety, as it always seems to do, because Mr. Maeng accepts Hajun's answer.

* * *

"I don't understand why living together is such a big deal. People already know you and Hajun were a thing," Sky says, popping another macaron into her mouth and speaking around it. "Like, the public doesn't know you're back together, but it's not like moving in together is weird for a couple." We've made a habit of meeting at a new cafe multiple times a week for breakfast or lunch, and today I tell her about the awkward meeting with the real estate agent. The soft background of cafe noise covers our quiet conversation.

"It's because of status and reputation. Living together as an unmarried couple... that's not done by people like me." I bite my lip. "But if I told my abba about wanting to be with Hajun seriously, he could punish him, remove him from the company for good—I can't do that to him." With Hajun staying in the company, my father has more power over us than if Hajun had to sign with another label.

In the past year, Abba has arranged several more blind dates with eligible lawyers and businessmen, none of which I have gone to. He's stopped scheduling them. My father expects me to live with him until I'm married. But I can't wait any longer.

"So you're still going to do it and keep it secret?" Sky questions. "How? What about that bodyguard your dad has follow you around?" She sneaks a glance at the opposite corner of the cafe, where a giant man named Gwan Jung in a hoodie and jeans sips his own coffee and watches the room.

Ever since the scandal, Abba has assigned me a full-time bodyguard who often accompanies me whenever I'm in public for my protection. Even now, my bodyguard watches me.

It's been another difficult adjustment, getting used to Gwan Jung. He's a nice man, despite his appearance. But I haven't even had a personal driver since high school, so having a bodyguard with me every time I leave the house or the office makes dating Hajun and keeping it a secret from my father, who my bodyguard reports to, a lot more challenging.

But Hajun and I are already making careful preparations to hide our living arrangement. "I'm going to rent a smaller place in an adjacent complex that shares the same parking structure. For all anyone else will know, I'm just moving out on my own."

"Ha. Can I sublet? Nevermind, I probably can't afford it." Sky pouts and slurps her pumpkin spice latte. She hardly ever gets the same drink twice.

"Sure. I'll give you a best friend discount. Your current place in Itaewon is too far for your commute, anyway."

Sky backtracks, holding her hands up as if to fend me off. "No, I was joking! I can't let you pay my rent!"

Just then, something occurs to me. I tip my head to the side, thinking. "Why not? You can be my cover for living with Hajun. You'd be helping me."

The small amount of satisfaction I get from this idea quickly sours. No matter how carefully mine and Hajun's life together is planned, the truth remains that we must hide our love for one another like a shameful secret.

KOSMIC FOREVER

HAJUN

The look on Aera's face from the realtor's questioning haunts me as I try to sleep at my single apartment in the company dorms. The whole situation twists and pulls my heart in too many directions.

How can I ask her to marry me without her father's permission? How can I live with her without guilt if I cannot marry her as she deserves?

There are too many eyes, too many rules.

All I know is that I cannot be the reason for her pain any longer. I must do what I should have done before. And I must do it without her knowing.

Because if she knew, she would stop me.

KOSMIC FOREVER

AERA

A week later, I sip a glass of champagne as I watch Hajun stow our bags in the storage compartment of the private jet. "Remind me again why you need me to come with you on a work trip?"

He had asked me to go with him to the airport this morning. Since it was Hajun, I cleared my schedule, but now he won't tell me any details—only that it's for "work," which I highly doubt. Hajun booked one of CKM's private jets, which are usually reserved for business trips for executives and artists. Considering the approval process it has to go through, I'm not sure how he managed it.

Hajun shuts the compartment door and turns to me with a smirk. "Maybe I need a hot manager to encourage my productivity."

A laugh bubbles in my throat with the alcohol. "So you're still not telling me where we're going."

"It's a surprise." He sinks into the seat facing mine, leaning his chin on his hand while he gazes at me.

"Right. I hate surprises."

"Hmm," he hums, an amused sound deep in his throat. "But I know the kind of surprises you do like."

I blush, but because of the presence of the flight crew through the open cockpit door, preparing for takeoff, I play along with the idea that this trip is "business related." "If you would tell me details, I might be able to assist you with your work. If you don't, I could find out easily with a single phone call—"

"Don't you dare." Hajun pins me with his gaze. "I want you to think of nothing else but me for the next nine hours."

My blush deepens. "So egotistical."

Hajun shrugs one shoulder, a smirk still playing at his lips. "I'm not famous for no reason. I have a right to be egotistical."

With the passenger area of the private jet to ourselves, and the flight attendant behind the privacy screen in the jumpseat near the cockpit, we sit beside each other. I spend the first few hours of the flight with my head on Hajun's shoulder and our hands tangled together on his thigh. We talk, Hajun sings snippets of songs for me in his smooth voice. The loud hum of the engine wraps us in a cocoon of peace.

Even if this trip is just an excuse for me to spend time with Hajun, I welcome it. Buying the villa is one step closer toward building the life we want together, even if we must hide that we are living together. Sky finally caved and agreed to be my fake roommate, subletting the luxury apartment from me for a miniscule fraction of what it's worth. If she knew how much I was actually paying for it, she would probably have a heart attack. Now I can tell abba that I'm moving in with her, even if it's not the truth.

But there is still a shard of pain in my chest at the fact that we have to keep it secret. Despite our efforts to ignore that obvious fact, it creeps into our every interaction like a shadow. Even peaceful ones like this.

"Hajun," I whisper, the lingering fear getting the better of me. "Are we doing the wrong thing?"

His fingers stop stroking the back of my hand. "What do you mean?" he asks, a note of uncertainty in his voice.

"I mean, if we're found out to be living together, that's another scandal. I don't want that for you." I swallow. Always the same worries with us. I wouldn't blame him if he didn't want to deal with that anymore.

Hajun pulls his hand from mine and turns to look at me, a muscle jumping in his jaw as he considers my words. "We both know who suffered more from that scandal," he says, anger flashing in his eyes. "This time I'm going to protect you. I don't want you to worry about that ever again."

"But how—"

He puts his index finger gently over my lips, cutting me off. "You're worrying about other things. That's not allowed." His eyes spark as he leans closer. "What can I do to make you think about just me, princess?"

I don't resist as his hand moves to cup my jaw, his lips tracing over mine. My mouth parts, letting him in, as my eyes close. The warmth of his mouth and the coaxing strokes of his tongue against mine blot out the rest of the universe for several blissful moments. I sigh, sinking my fingers into the hair at the back of his head, pulling him closer.

He chuckles against my mouth and drops his hand from my jaw to trace my arm, my waist, my thigh, bunching my dress beneath his fist. I gasp as his hand slips higher.

"We're not alone!" I remind him, pulling away to glance toward the privacy screen at the front of the plane, behind which the flight attendant sits.

"The engine is loud, if you can be quiet," Hajun whispers

with a wicked smirk, as his fingers slip inside my underwear, sliding between my legs and finding the most sensitive part of me with ease.

His thumb begins stroking in gentle circles, making my head fall back against the headrest of my seat. He watches me closely beneath hooded eyelids as my breath comes fast and shallow. Pleasure quakes through my body from the epicenter of my thighs. I struggle to muffle my gasps, so I press my face into the warmth of his shoulder as a wave of pleasure crashes over me. He continues the steady movement of his fingers, causing aftershocks to ripple through me.

Hajun withdraws his hand and smirks at me. "Feeling better, princess?"

I shoot him a challenging look, not willing to let him off the hook. "Your turn."

The smirk falls from his face, replaced with that hooded-eyed look as he watches me unbuckle my seatbelt and kneel on the floor between his knees. After unbuckling his seatbelt, I unbutton and unzip his pants, and his erection springs free, smooth and hot when I take it in my hands. I lean over his lap and close my mouth over the sensitive tip, causing him to shudder and cup the back of my head, stroking my hair. "And to think you were protesting a moment ago."

"Shut up," I say. My mouth moves over him, taking him as deep into my throat as I can, tongue massaging his shaft before pulling back.

A soft, deep moan is torn from Hajun's throat as he squeezes his eyes shut. "Aera," he breathes, his head falling back against the seat just as mine had.

I hum in satisfaction as I bob my head. There's a certain thrill that goes through me at the thought that the flight attendant might overhear. I'm so sick of trying to keep us secret that I hunger for acts of rebellion like this.

Hajun gasps my name and comes into my mouth with a groan loud enough that I actually worry the flight attendant might have heard. I swallow the warm liquid that explodes into my mouth, then wipe my mouth with the back of my hand and grin up at him. "I win."

He looks at me through a gaze narrowed with drowsy pleasure. "We'll see about that, princess. Now please put your seatbelt back on."

KOSMIC FOREVER

HAJUN

We land in the Republic of Maldives around dinnertime, stepping off the plane into balmy air with a pleasant salty-sea breeze, a contrast with the chilly autumn air back in Korea. The Maldives is a small nation of islands in the Indian Ocean. Aera quickly finds out where we are when we present our passports to immigration.

She squints at me in suspicion as we leave the airport in a taxi. "Are we on vacation, Hajun?"

"Yes," I admit, smirking, "I lied. But you would never agree to go with me if I hadn't."

She shakes her head, smiling. She was never fooled.

We arrive at the harbor after a taxi ride, where we board a private boat that will take us to our destination. The boat's captain is a friendly, older South Asian man. Aera stands at the railing, staring out at the sapphire blue ocean stretching out around us, as the late afternoon sun shimmers upon it. I come up behind her and wrap my arms around her waist to steady her as the boat rocks beneath us. There's no one to watch us who cares.

"Are you mad?" I ask, resting my chin on top of her head.

"Very," she teases. "I canceled some important meetings for you." Her shoulders are loose, posture relaxed for the first time in a long while.

We needed this.

A short while later, the boat pulls up to a private wooden dock, where the boat captain helps us unload our baggage. I lead Aera along the dock over the water. Upon a short strip of white sandy beach, a small wood-thatched bungalow, framed by a strand of lush green jungle, sits on stilts above the water. Not a single other building or human in sight, just an oasis in the middle of the sea.

"You did this?" Aera asks in disbelief, gazing around at our private paradise.

"For you." I find the key where the owner of the place left it, tucked inside a wooden carving of a sea turtle between several potted plants on the deck. I let us inside the bungalow, which has a large bed, a small but luxurious bathroom, and a small kitchen with a stocked fridge. The living room is a deck above the water with shutters that can be closed in a rainshower.

Dinner awaits us on the deck in ceramic covered dishes—lobster, fish curry and still-warm flatbread, fresh coconut, juicy mangoes, and sweet taro in coconut milk for dessert. As we eat, the sun is sinking toward the horizon, painting gold and pink colors over turquoise water. The only sound is the peaceful lapping of waves against the shore.

"That was the best food I've ever had. I want to swim but I can't, I'm so full," Aera groans, moving over to the loveseat nearby and collapsing onto it to watch the sunset. I sit beside her, and she curls into my side, my arm around her. "Thank you for this," she adds quietly. I kiss the side of her head in reply.

We sit in silence together on the deck over the water watching the sun disappear into the ocean, the stars twinkling in the now-dark sky. It is only after a small choked noise comes from Aera's throat, that I realize she's crying.

"What's wrong?" I ask in alarm, swiping a tear off of her cheek.

She turns her face up to mine, her brown eyes holding a sheen of tears. "I'm so happy to be with you, Hajun," she manages to get out. "I wish we could stay here forever. And never go back to Seoul, where we have to hide who we are to each other."

I can feel my heart cracking in two. "I don't want to hide."

"But we have to." Her voice is so tired.

"Maybe we don't." I hold her gaze. "Come with me, I want to show you something."

KOSMIC FOREVER

AERA

Hajun takes my hand in his and leads me down the wooden steps that wrap around the bungalow, onto the white sand. Neither of us are wearing shoes, and the sand is surprisingly soft beneath my feet. We walk side by side down the small beach. The moon is a silvery crescent, and the stars are now shining brightly overhead, without city lights to dim their brilliance. I've lived so long in cities that I've forgotten how beautiful the stars are.

"What did you want to show me?" I ask Hajun. Maybe he simply wanted to remind me that in this tiny island paradise, at least for one night, we don't have to hide.

"Look at the waves."

I look down at the gentle waves rolling onto the wet sand near our feet, coming close enough that one of them reaches my toes, the water warmer than I expected. At first I see nothing out of the ordinary. Then, a blue shimmer catches my eye. As I peer more closely, the water breaks onto the shore. its edges ripple with pinpricks of glowing neon blue. The longer I watch, the brighter it flickers, the waves along the shore almost like a reflection of the starlight in the sky.

"Oh, it's bioluminescent plankton." With delight, I remember learning about it before. I never thought I would see it with my own eyes. Wonderingly, I look at Hajun, who is standing with his hands in his pockets a couple feet away and a strange look shining in his eyes as he gazes at me. With only the light of the moon, the stars and the sparkling waves to see, I can't read his expression well. "Hajun?"

He sucks in a deep breath. "Aera."

"Hajun?" I echo, sensing from his usage of my real name instead of my nickname that he's about to tell me something. Apprehension makes my heart race.

Holding my gaze, Hajun sinks onto the sand before me. My heartbeat stumbles when I realize he is on one knee, and that he has something in his hands. "Aera," he repeats.

I feel dizzy, as if I can feel the planet spinning a thousand kilometers an hour beneath my feet.

"I would not have made it to debut if it weren't for meeting you. There has not been a single love song that I have written without thinking of you. And the year I spent apart from you was harder than anything else, even leaving the group. I want to be by your side, not in secret but in the light. Aera, will you marry me?"

KOSMIC FOREVER

HAJUN: A WEEK BEFORE

"Chairman Kim will see you now."

I followed the secretary to the double doors to the CKM Entertainment CEO's office, as he opened one for me and gestured me inside. My heart thumped wildly in my chest. Never had I been more nervous—not at my audition, not during monthly evaluations as a trainee, not even on stage in front of tens of thousands of fans. I straightened my spine and entered.

Aera's father sat behind his giant desk like a king in a throne room, his face a mask of cool indifference. He could end my contract with the company for what I was about to ask of him. He might have already if Aera hadn't convinced him to let me stay in the company as a solo act. But I saw no other way.

"Yun Hajun. What do you want?"

I kept my eyes fixed to the floor. "I'm here to apologize, sir. And to ask that you consider what I'm about to say."

His voice is a dangerous rumble. "Go on, then."

"I apologize for how my actions have impacted this company, and your family. I wish to make reparations now and do what I should have done when I realized how deeply I care for your daughter."

The chairman held up a hand, stopping me from saying more. "Name your price," he said.

I anticipated this. Holding his gaze, I said, "Respectfully, sir, there's no amount of money in the world that would make me stop loving your daughter. Which is why I'm here to humbly ask you this." I dropped to my knees, kneeling in front of his desk. "I ask that you give me your blessing so that I may propose marriage to Kim Aera. I am not a man from a respected family, as you might wish your daughter's husband to be. But I have created my own fortune through hard work at your company, and her happiness is my only desire. Please, let me marry Kim Aera so that I may be her devoted husband for the rest of my life."

KOSMIC FOREVER

AERA: NOW

The vertigo of this moment steals the breath from my chest.

I haven't thought of marriage with a single spark of hope since my mother died. In fact, I dread the whole affair. It's my fate to marry for social standing.

Yet, here is the man I love kneeling before me, asking me to choose him of my own will. To tie our lives together. To be by each other's side, not in secret but in the light.

He knows all too well the potential consequences of such a choice. I know it, too.

And I know what my heart chooses.

"Yes, I will marry you," I reply.

KOSMIC FOREVER

HAJUN

I can't breathe.

Aera extends her left hand to me, trembling just a little.

I open the ring box, the star-shaped diamond on its white gold band catching the light just enough to shine through the darkness. With my chest cracking open, I slide the ring onto Aera's finger, where another gleam of starlight sparks from it.

She sinks onto the sand and throws her arms around my neck, pressing her lips to mine. Wrapping my arms around her, I can't believe this moment is real. I kiss her back slowly, gently, taking my time now that I know we have all the time in the world. Her lips taste like salt from tears on her cheeks.

A wave reaches us, soaking the legs of my pants and the hem of her dress. I break away from our kiss to slide one arm beneath her legs and the other around her lower back, picking her up.

Aera laughs as I carry her back toward the bungalow. "I can walk, you know."

"You're going to have to get used to me carrying you, princess. I plan on doing this for a very long time."

I set her down on her feet once inside the bungalow, where she grabs my hand and tugs me to the bed. The only light comes from the lanterns on the deck, flames flickering against the darkness. Peeling off our wet, sandy clothes, she pulls me down on top of her. Propping myself up with my arms, I press kisses to her jaw and neck, moving lower to kiss her breasts. She sinks her hands into my hair and arches her body against mine as my mouth travels down her stomach, tasting her soft skin, making her gasp.

"Hajun," she whimpers, and I smile against her skin.

I move back up and lock eyes with hers. "Yes, princess?"

"I love you."

"I love you, too."

She wraps a hand around the base of my length and guides me to her opening. I sink deep into her warmth. Our bodies move together like waves against the shore, pulled by the gravity and the moon.

KOSMIC FOREVER

AERA

The dawn comes soft and breezy. Hajun wakes me with kisses all over my body that leave me breathless and make it hard to get out of bed. He holds me in his arms and we watch the sun rise through the open shutters.

Breakfast is brought by two women in a boat and left on the deck outside. The large wicker basket holds a dish containing a large omelet with tuna, curry leaves, and coconut rice, and a platter of fresh sliced dragon fruit and mango.

"I can't believe you arranged all of this to propose to me," I laugh, waving goodbye to the women who brought our breakfast.

"I had to get you away from your meetings somehow." Hajun winks, lounging on the chair across from mine and licking fruit juice off his fingers. His black hair is tousled, and he makes a white t-shirt and shorts look unbelievably good. "We have this place all to ourselves for one more night."

My chest tightens, and I set my fork back down. "Then we go back."

I've been trying not to think about it, but under the light of day I can't help but be reminded that choosing one another over everything else has its consequences.

He nods, and his brow furrows in that way that tells me he's debating whether to tell me something. "What is it?" I ask.

Hajun hesitates. "Could we wait to talk about this until tomorrow morning?"

"No." I know I'm ruining the mood, but the anxiety welling in me can only be ignored for so long.

"I asked your father for permission."

I blink. Whatever I was expecting, it wasn't that. "You... he knows?"

I can't even imagine it. My father letting Hajun go through with proposing to me. It goes against every plan he's ever made for me.

"More than that. He gave me his blessing." He runs his hand through his hair, avoiding my gaze.

There's something else. A catch.

There's always a catch, with my father.

"With the condition that he arrange a public wedding for us," Hajun finally admits. "With press and cameras."

My stomach drops. After the hatred and death threats I got from saesangs after the photo scandal, a publicized wedding sounds like a terrible idea. And yet, from Abba's perspective, it's the best way to salvage and leverage the situation to the company's advantage.

A public wedding is the last thing I want.

Hajun sees my distress and reaches across the table to grasp my hand. "Aera, I'm sorry—"

"How could you ask *him* for permission first? Like I'm not my own person?" I pull my hand away and push back from the table. "Just—I need some time." Turning away, I retreat down the steps to the beach and walk down the sandy stretch, alone.

KOSMIC FOREVER

HAJUN

I've fucked up. I fist my fingers in my hair, pressing the heels of my hands into my eyes as my chest cracks open.

How can I explain to Aera that asking her father was the only way I could do this without letting her down or destroying her family? Without losing my career? If I felt I could have asked her first without his permission, I would have.

I look to the beach, where Aera is standing in the waves.

KOSMIC FOREVER

AERA

I hear Hajun approach behind me on the beach. "I'm sorry," he says. "I wanted to make everything right, so that we wouldn't have to hide anymore. If you don't want to have the wedding, we can run away. I would do that for you. I would do anything for you."

My temper cooled in the ocean waves, I recognize his reasoning. But it still stings. "No, I'm sorry. I just... sometimes wish that these decisions were entirely my own."

"You don't need to apologize. It is your decision," Hajun says, and I hear him walk into the water behind me. He touches my arm lightly.

He's right. I said yes, ready to accept any consequences for the chance to be with him. But because of him, we don't have to give up anything. We can be together in the light. If that means enduring a bit of public spectacle, so be it.

I turn and his arms envelope me, my head fitting beneath his chin. "Let's do it," I say finally. "The wedding my abba wants."

"Are you sure?"

I nod. After all of this, he would still leave all of it with me if that's what I wanted. "I didn't think I could love you more than I already did," I murmur.

Hajun presses a kiss to the top of my head. I can hear the smile in his voice. "Nothing's impossible, princess."

"When I'm with you
　　There is no one else
　　I get heaven to myself"

— "The Astronaut," Jin

KOSMIC FOREVER

AERA

The day before my wedding, I visit my mother's grave.

On a hillside dappled with green trees and manicured shrubs is the cemetery where her ashes were laid to rest. I walk the winding path by myself, although my bodyguard trails behind me, always watching.

I stop before the stone headstone with her name. 강아름. Kang Areum.

A dull pain lances through the center of my chest. I kneel on the grass, placing the bundle of white flowers at the base of her headstone.

"Eomma," I say. "I'm getting married tomorrow."

The stone doesn't reply. But I keep talking, wishing that somehow, she'll be able to hear me.

"His name is Hajun. He's a singer, like you."

For a moment, I let myself recall things that I haven't allowed myself to think about for many years.

When I was little, my mother explained to that she wasn't supposed to marry my father. She was a ballad singer from a normal, working-class background who rose to fame because of her own talent. My father was the heir to CKM Group. It was like the plot of a drama. By chance, they met. They fell in love. And Abba refused to marry anyone else, going as far as to break off his engagement with a suitable chaebol heiress.

After my parents' marriage, he gave Eomma the funds to start CKM Entertainment. Of all of CKM Group's companies, my abba took it upon himself to take over as its full-time CEO when she passed away, not trusting anyone else to run it properly. Even though becoming CEO of CKM Ent. spread him much too thin along with his other duties, it seemed that the only way he could deal with his sorrow was to work even harder.

He never spoke of her after her death, but I knew that losing her had broken him. It was because of this that Abba put so much pressure on me. In order to maintain our social status, I would have to make up for what he failed to do. Even though we were still chaebol, there was a stain on our name. Somehow, he thought he could save me from heartbreak by forcing me into the role of a perfect heir. I resent him for it, but I also understand.

I don't miss the irony that if CKM Entertainment had never been founded, I never would have met Hajun.

"I guess I have you to thank for all of this," I say. Tears unspool from the corners of my eyes and streak down my cheeks. "I never thought I would be happy again. But I think... if I can get through this... I might be."

* * *

"How are you feeling?" Sky murmurs, leaning over me as she blends makeup across my cheeks.

My stomach flips over as I catch my own eyes in the vanity mirror. My composure is cracked, a panic in my gaze that I can't seem to disguise. Not only am I getting married today, but the event will be incredibly public—parts of it will even be broadcast on national television.

With the public spectacle of marriage, the scandal of a chaebol heiress dating and an idol will become a romantic story that the public can respect. At least, that's the idea.

But after what happened when the scandal broke—the death threats, the vilification of me on social media—I am terrified to be back in the spotlight.

At least my best friend is the one helping me get ready for my wedding. As a professional stylist, Sky has taken over everything from helping me put on my dress to doing my makeup and hair. We were able to get the other staff to leave, if only for a moment. So at least for now, it's just us here in the bridal suite.

"I'm going to need a drink to get through this," I mumble.

Sky laughs. "That can be arranged. In fact, I brought something." She goes over to her suitcase in the corner, unzips it, and holds up a glass bottle of tequila with a mischievous smile. "One shot for each of us. For courage. No more than that. We don't need you stumbling down the aisle."

We obtain a couple of crystal glass tumblers from the minibar, pour a small amount into each, and take our shots together. For a moment, we're back in college, trying to distract ourselves from our mountains of homework by getting drunk and doing nothing for a few hours.

Then reality hits me again.

"Hey," Sky says, grabbing my shoulders and looking me in the eyes. "You're going to be great."

I nod, because I will be. When all of this is over, when Hajun and I can finally be together.

KOSMIC FOREVER

HAJUN

"What a pleasure it is to meet you," says an older woman who is some distant relation of Aera's, though her tone does not match her words. She's dressed in a designer dress and the excess of diamonds on her neck and wrists catch the light of the reception hall and pierce my eyes with every movement. Her husband beside her bestows the white envelope with the cash gift. I thank them before they leave me and head through the entrance to the ballroom. Their names slip from my mind as soon as the next group of guests approaches.

That couple were probably in the two-hundreds of guests I've had to greet today. My throat is dry from speaking formalities to so many people, but life as an idol has prepared me for this. Mostly.

This venue is one of the most expensive in Seoul. It features a hotel, a ballroom with floor-to-ceiling glass windows where the ceremony will take place, and a large veranda overlooking the Seoul skyline where the reception will be held. Aera's father—my boss—spared no expense for our wedding.

Mr. Kim, Aera's father, was here, until a few minutes ago when he excused himself and disappeared. My mother and grandfather, Eomma and Harabeoji, are here greeting people as well. As much as I've tried to shield them from my life as an idol, they are in the spotlight today, in the media but also among South Korea's elite, including members of Aera's extended family. Eomma was worried about choosing a dress that would mark her as lower class, so I spent what would have been, during my childhood, six months' rent on her clothing for today. She wears a custom-made, elegant modern take on a traditional hanbok, in fine fabric the color of the sea in Jeju. She glows with pride and shows no strain at all, despite her worries leading up to this day.

Worlds are colliding—public and private, mine and Aera's. Nothing in my life could have prepared me for such a life-changing event. I can hardly believe it's real.

Most of all, while I greet yet another guest, what I'm thinking of is Aera. She's likely nearly done with her hair and makeup. Though she has assured me many times that this is what she wants, I would abandon all of this world for her in a heartbeat.

Or so I think, but the next group includes six familiar faces who remind me why leaving the world of the Korean music industry would be as hard as abandoning my own family. They immediately crush me into a group hug that leaves me laughing and wincing a little in pain. I feel one of the first genuine smiles of the day spread across my face.

My former bandmates in KOSMIC know how to make an entrance.

"Congratulations, brother," Changmin tells me, the words echoed by the sincerity in his eyes.

"Congratulations." Tai grips my arm a moment longer, the last to let go. "Be happy," he says, so much love and weight in those simple words.

"I will," I promise, smiling back at him.

Jaesung thrusts his cash envelope at me, obviously eager to give it to me. "Hyung, you look so cool in that suit. I think I want to get married now."

Simon snorts, following our maknae's wide-eyed gaze to Changmin's little sister, about the same age as Jaesung, a trainee at CKM, and very pretty, currently standing with their parents speaking to my family. "Don't even think about it."

The KOSMIC members are accompanied by their own families. Haru's mother gives me a hug, followed by a back thumping from Jaesung's father and congratulations and laughter from the other families.

I lean on the courage my members' presence brings me as the final guests begin to arrive, and the ceremony approaches.

KOSMIC FOREVER

AERA

Months ago, not long after Hajun proposed, Abba and I took a weekend trip to Jeju to meet Hajun's family.

The experience was odd, partly as I cannot recall taking any sort of vacation with my father before, but also because of how out of place at Hajun's mother's cozy house in Jeju, drinking barley tea, chuckling with Hajun's grandfather, and complimenting his mother's cooking.

For the first time in a long time, I felt as if I could have a real family again.

* * *

Sky walks with me to the reception room fifteen minutes before the ceremony, led by a staff member down some back corridors so that we don't run into anyone on the way.

When we reach the reception room, though, my father is waiting. He sits on one of the armchairs with a glass of whiskey in his hand, looking out of place among the comfortable furniture and throw pillows on either side of him. When we come in, he sets the glass down on a nearby table.

"I'll, uh, let you be alone," Sky says in English, backing awkwardly out of the room and shutting the door behind her.

Abba takes in my wedding dress with a measured gaze. The champagne-toned dress is floor-length with an A-line figure, off-the-shoulder short sleeves, and a full shimmery tulle skirt that catches the light when I move. My short hair is covered by a veil of the same fabric. The dress, like every part of this wedding, must have cost a fortune.

"You look beautiful," he finally says.

"Thanks," I murmur, and cross the room to perch on the couch across from him, arranging my full skirts around me the best that I can. The clock on the wall shows that it's fifteen minutes until the ceremony. The ticking sound it makes is hard to ignore in the silence.

Abba meets my eyes. "I have something to tell you."

I don't know what he could possibly want to tell me at this moment, but a couple wild thoughts swirl through my mind at the same time. He's started dating someone, he's sick, or—and this is absurd—he's decided to call off the wedding at the last minute.

"I've decided to step down as CEO of CKM Entertainment," he states. "And I want you to take over."

The world tilts beneath me. It takes me a moment to find my voice. "You want me to be CEO?"

"I'll still be on the board of directors, but you would be the executive officer directly overseeing the company," he explains patiently, as if that's the part I don't understand.

That is a lot of power to give to a 25-year-old. He could easily appoint someone else with more experience. "Why?" I ask, bewildered.

"Because the company needs the leadership of a young, forward-thinking CEO. It needs your leadership. You already have many ideas, and I want to give you the power to execute them."

Abba speaks these words in his usual steady, unaffected manner, and yet, it hits me that this is a profound gesture of love on his part. That all of this, even the public wedding to Hajun, was leading up to him passing the company on to me.

What could I do with so much power? He's right, I have ideas—ways that I would like to change the K-Pop industry— that until now were only that. Now I would have the power to make those changes happen.

Starting with Hajun.

He would be able to rejoin KOSMIC.

Tears pricking my eyes, I throw my arms around my father and hug him. "Thank you, Abba."

He returns my embrace. "Don't cry. You'll ruin your makeup."

I laugh, because he remains ever practical. But I steady myself, stopping my tears from leaving my eyes.

A knock sounds on the door, and the lead event organizer pokes her head in. "It's time."

My heart leaps into my throat.

KOSMIC FOREVER

HAJUN

The hotel's grand ballroom is divided by a single walkway leading to a stage, with neatly arranged chairs on either side. Hundreds of people sit at these chairs, beneath a constellation of tiny amber lights strung from the ceiling to look like stars. A set of classical musicians sit to the side of the stage, where they play an elegant arrangement.

The ceremony begins with Eomma and Harabeoji walking down the elevated walkway. Then, they take their seats in the first row. Eomma's poise and Harabeoji's dignity give me the courage to walk through the entrance to the ballroom onto the walkway, with all of the lights shining down upon me, my heart thundering in my chest.

Time blurs, and suddenly I am on stage at my own concert. My strides gain their familiar confidence. At the end of the walkway is the stage where the Master of Ceremony awaits. My steps carry me there and I take my place, then look to the entrance.

I can hardly breathe as the music swells and Aera walks through the doors.

Her chin is held high, a soft and calm smile upon her face

even as cameras flash. She's glowing like the sun as she holds my gaze across the room.

I love her so much I could fall to my knees right there.

Mr. Kim walks arm in arm with his daughter, and as they reach the dais he meets my eyes and holds them for a beat, as if holding me to a silent promise. I bow my head.

Aera joins me standing before the Master of Ceremony, and her father steps down from the stage to sit in the front row.

The Master of Ceremony clears his throat as the music quiets. "We are gathered here today to witness the uniting of Yun Hajun and Kim Aera. Do you, Yun Hajun, swear to take Kim Aera as your lawfully wedded wife, to have and to hold, for better, or for worse, for richer or for poorer, in sickness and in health, to love and to cherish, till death do you part?"

Aera gives me a small smile, her eyes sparkling. She is my entire universe.

"I do."

KOSMIC FOREVER

AERA

Hajun stands before me, unbelievably handsome in his midnight black suit and tie, holding my gaze as if nothing else matters but the two of us. For a moment, I forget that we are on stage in front of an entire crowd of onlookers, in front of press with cameras.

"Do you, Kim Aera, swear to take Yun Hajun as your lawfully wedded husband, to have and to hold, for better, or for worse, for richer or for poorer, in sickness and in health, to love and to cherish, till death do you part?"

I nod. "I do." With my whole heart.

"Please exchange rings."

Hajun withdraws a ring from his pocket, the same ring with which he proposed to me on the beach, with its glittering rhombus-shaped diamond. At the same time, I pull a white-gold band from the tiny, concealed pouch attached to my bouquet. The band has a tiny rhombus-shaped diamond embedded in the band, a mirror to my own ring.

Taking a steadying breath, I slip my band onto his finger, then lift my eyes to his. I feel him take my hands in his own. He slowly slides his ring onto my left hand, but doesn't let go of my hands or break my gaze.

"You may kiss the bride."

Hajun leans down to kiss me, a soft and lingering brush of his lips against my own as his arms encircle my waist. Not recalling the eyes or cameras on us, I grab his tie and kiss him back.

When we separate, we turn hand in hand and bow deeply to the audience. My face is flushed, and my heart feels like it might burst, as we leave the stage together.

Hajun's Harabeoji greets us in the foyer along with his Eomma. Eomma wraps me in a tight hug as soon as she sees me, while Harabeoji weeps quietly, telling Hajun how proud he is to watch his grandson's wedding.

"I am so happy to welcome you as my daughter," Eomma tells me as she pulls away.

Abba stands to the side, watching us all. I don't hesitate but rush into his arms, and he is smiling when the cameraman takes a picture of the five of us together as a family.

When pictures are done, we join our guests on the veranda for the reception. Dinner has already been served, a banquet of traditional and modern dishes. I opt for tender lobster meat and honeyed rice with nuts, while Hajun gets a big plate with beef short ribs. We sit at a table with our closest family and friends. With Sky's help, I finally take off my veil so that it doesn't get in the way of eating.

"You didn't seem nervous at all," Sky reassures me. "The ceremony was beautiful."

"Thanks." I let out a breath. The ceremony had gone smoothly. No one shouted questions at us — the journalists covering the event were told that they would be escorted out if they did.

"This party is insane. I think I've seen five celebrities," Sky says around a big bite of her food.

"You're not excited to see us?" Byunho asks her with a teasing smirk.

Sky swallows, looking flustered. "I see you like every day," she mumbles.

The rest of the afternoon passes by in a blur. I greet guests I wasn't able to see before the wedding and stretch my memory to recall the names of all of CKM Group's partners and their families.

KOSMIC forces us to take a picture with them. I'm not sure whose idea it was, but it's happening before I can protest.

Jaesung puts his arm around my shoulders despite the fact that he has to lean down to do it, then makes me laugh by making a goofy face, while Haru gives an oblivious Simon bunny ears. Byunho pulls a dark pair of sunglasses from somewhere and makes a rock-on sign like he's posing at a red carpet. Changmin throws up a peace sign, while Hajun has his arms slung over both his and Tai's shoulders. Sky snaps the photo, laughing at their antics.

I notice Byunho watching Sky as she pretends not to notice.

Tai comes up to talk to me after the photo. I expected him to seem sad today, but he only gives me a slight smile. "You're right for each other. I wish you happiness."

"Thank you."

I look around to find that Hajun has disappeared. "Have you seen Hajun?" I ask Changmin, but he only winks.

Hajun reappears moments later on a stage, holding an acoustic guitar and no longer wearing his suit jacket. As the sun sets behind him over the Seoul skyline and mountains, purple and pink clouds blending with golden light, he performs the song he wrote for me to a hushed crowd. My heart aches. His voice is the most beautiful thing I've ever heard.

KOSMIC FOREVER

HAJUN

Though I'm performing in front of an audience, there is only one person I'm performing for. I hold Aera's gaze as I sing first one song that I wrote for her, and then another, a new song that no one has ever heard before. Where better to debut my new single than at my own wedding?

When I've finished, I come down from the stage, go to her and offer her my hand. "Will you dance with me?" I ask, raising my brows with a grin.

"I can hardly say no, can I?" she says, but she stands and lets me draw her onto the dance floor. My members have taken my place on stage—Tai on drums, Byunho and Changmin on electric guitars, Simon on piano, Jaesung on bass, and Haru doing main vocals—to play one of our slower, ballad songs that's already arranged for live band performance at our concerts.

I pull Aera close and guide her through the steps of a waltz. "This reminds me of something," she says, her head near my shoulder. "When you were a trainee, you insulted my dancing skills."

"Insult?" I smirk. "No, your lack of coordination is one of my favorite things about you."

She steps on my foot, rather harder than I think is an accident.

"Ow. If I recall correctly, I believe I may have also pointed out how much I admire your brilliance and work ethic. Now that you're my wife, I will have to remind you daily."

She snorts and pulls away to smile at me. Eyes soft, she whispers, "I love you."

My heart still skips a beat whenever I hear her say that. "And I love you."

KOSMIC FOREVER

AERA

The audience throws pale pink rose petals into the air on the sidewalk outside the hotel, waving at us as we leave. A barricade prevents paparazzi who weren't invited to the event from getting close to us, and I do my best to block out their shouted questions as we reach the white limousine that will take us to the airport. I've changed from my wedding dress into a royal purple dress that is elegant yet comfortable for travel. This time, I'm the one surprising Hajun with the secret destination of Bali for our week-long honeymoon.

When we come back to Seoul, everything will be different. We'll live together in our beautiful villa with a view of the Han River. We'll no longer have to hide our love for each other from anyone. And I still haven't told him— after Abba steps down and I take his place as the CEO of CKM, Hajun will be able to rejoin KOSMIC, which I know he wants but doesn't dare hope for.

As soon as Hajun slides into the limousine after me, I wrap my arms around his neck and kiss him slowly. "Finally, I get heaven to myself," he murmurs, only reluctantly letting go of me so that we can put our seatbelts on. We sit beside each other, hands entwined. The limousine is moving forward now, toward the airport, and with the divider down between us and the driver, we have privacy for the first time in weeks.

"I need to tell you something," I say.

Hajun instantly recognizes my serious tone and stares at me with a slight expression of alarm, as if wondering if I'm about to tell him he's going to be a father.

Actually, that's one of the rumors that is going around the internet as the reason behind our wedding. But it's not true. I don't think either of us are in any hurry to be parents yet.

"I'm going to be CEO of CKM. My father told me today."

He blinks. "Oh." A flirtatious smirk curves his lips. "Well, since you're already the boss of me, that won't change much."

I shake my head, laughing at his inability to take anything seriously. "Don't you see what that means? You'll get to go back to KOSMIC. Isn't that what you wanted, more than anything?"

Hajun shakes his head, the smirk disappearing. "I do want to be a member of KOSMIC again. But you should understand that my career, you being CEO, those things don't matter nearly as much to me." He cups the side of my face with his hand. "What I wanted more than anything was to be with you forever."

My heart flutters as if my chest is filled with butterflies. The hopeful kind. "Well, lucky you," I whisper as I lean in to kiss him again. "Because this time I'm not going anywhere."

THE END

A life, a sparkle in your eyes
Heaven coming through
And I love you"

—"The Astronaut," Jin

ACKNOWLEDGMENTS

When I published my first book, *Kosmic Heart*, I wasn't sure anyone would read it. It's not a perfect book, but it did come from my heart when I was in a very difficult place in my life. The fact that so many people loved it was so much more than I hoped for.

Kosmic Kiss was a harder book to write. I knew I had to give my readers something new, and I struggled with the plot for this book for a while. It's been almost two full years since *Kosmic Heart* was released, and finally, KOSMIC is making a comeback.

I wouldn't have been able to write this book without you, my readers, KOSMIC's Infinities, writing reviews and commenting on social media to tell me that you couldn't wait to read it. It's cliche, but a lot of what Changmin said in his speech to Infinities at the concert is also from me in a way. So I'll leave you with his words.

"It's been a long journey to be here together. We're very thankful to you for standing by us even when there are hardships, or even though you've had to wait for us for a long time. We know how much you have done for us. We don't know yet everything that the future will hold, but we promise to keep working hard for you. Thank you."